MW00904101

THE MARRIAGE THAT DIDN'T STAY IN VEGAS

Phoenix Rayne

This is a work of fiction. Names, characters, businesses, places, events, and incidents either are the products of the author's imagination or used in a fictitious manner. Any resemblance to actual persons, living or dead, or actual events is purely coincidental.

© 2015 Phoenix Rayne. All rights are reserved. Unauthorized reproduction, in any manner, is prohibited.

Published by Ambiance Books

The sun was beaming on my face and my head was swimming. I couldn't tell if I was on the floor or the bed. I stared up at the ceiling, afraid to move too quickly.

"What the hell did I drink last night?" I asked myself.

I heard someone stirring nearby.

"Hello?" I called out.

Someone moved again.

I held my breath as I realized someone else was breathing in the room with me. "Hello, is someone there?"

A groan came from below.

I slowly tried to get up. I soon realized that I was on the floor and I wasn't on the bed. Well, I was on the bed, but a body laid between the bed and me. Wait, I'm still not telling you this right. I was laying on somebody. His chest was as hard as stone and ripples were deep. With a body this tan and toned, he had to be a stripper.

Shit! I've screwed a stripper. I looked down and oh yes; I had been rode, hard from the looks of it. I slid out of the bed as quietly as I could, held on to the cream color sheets as tightly as possible and saw my weave piece draped over the bedside lamp. I snatched it and then went in search of my clothes. I found a heel under the bed, my panties under the window, and my dress in one of the corners. Now all I needed was my other shoe, my bra, and my purse. I looked over the bedroom and found nothing. I looked over towards the bathroom and saw my other shoe. I snatched it up quickly. I searched the bedroom all the way over again and still nothing.

In the sitting area, I saw my bra hanging from the ceiling fan with no way I could reach it. I went to the wall and turned on every switch. All of the lights came on and the curtains opened wide. The ceiling fan didn't move an inch.

"Shit!" I yelled a little too loudly.

I froze, but I didn't hear the stripper stir. I saw my clutch on the counter and grabbed it. I dropped the sheet and got dressed, still braless. I tried a few more switches and still nothing but more lights.

I walked to the front door and stopped. If I'd had sex with this man, I at least needed to know his damn name. I looked around the big room and didn't find a sock, a shirt, not anything belonging to a man. I tiptoed back into the bedroom, and the stripper was still lying flat on his back buck-naked.

Dear God, what a body…

I definitely did not want him waking up and seeing this train wreck. I found a white, button-down shirt, a pair of cuff links, and socks. No pants, no wallet, and no cell phone were insight. I saw some black fabric underneath the stripper and I cringed.

"Shit," I whispered this time.

I had to get the fabric from under him. I was almost certain it was a pair of pants. I tugged and nothing; I pulled again and he stirred a little. I kneeled down on the bed quietly and slowly. I tried to push him, but he wasn't budging. I yanked at the fabric one last time and he was still knocked out.

"Screw the pants," I whispered.

I turned to get off the bed, but a pair of the lightest brown eyes I had ever seen yanked me back down. They were the color of honey and I was mesmerized. He pulled me down on top of him, and then he rolled us both over. He towered over me while he kissed my neck.

"Phoebe," he whispered in my ear.

I was in utter shock. *The stripper knew my name, my real name.*

By the time I collected myself, he was snoring again. It took me forever to get from under him, but I finally made it. Once I was freed from Conan's grip, I bolted.

Screw those pants and this stripper.

I grabbed the rest of my shit and ran to the front door.

"Pheb?" he called from the bedroom.

I swung the door wide open and dropped one of my heels on the floor. I bent over to pick it up and saw a piece of paper that had been slid underneath the door. I opened it quickly: a bill. I shoved it in my purse and ran down the hallway.

When I stepped off the elevator, my heels clicked against the marble floor as I walked. I saw the ladies' room and headed in that direction. I got a few stares but nothing major. When I looked in the bathroom mirror, I gasped. I looked like shit, and I scared myself. Two older women walked in and gave me a once over. Both of them went into stalls. I scrubbed my face free of smudged makeup.

My phone rang from inside my purse.

"Hello?" I answered.

"Where are you? We woke up, and you're not here," she yawned.

"Addison, what the hell happened last night?" I scowled.

"What?"

"I woke up in bed with a stripper!"

One of the ladies was out of her stall and washing her hands now. She stared at in me in utter shock with her mouth slightly agape.

I grabbed my purse and walked out of the bathroom. "Hold on a sec."

As soon as I turned the corner, I saw the stripper at the front desk. He wore a pair of black pants and a t-shirt. The concierge was pointing towards the bathroom and the stripper was coming my way. I ran down the side hall and entered the kitchen area. The cooks stared, but no one said anything. A couple of them pointed towards the exit and then kept right on cooking. I guess they saw shit like this all the time. I went out the back door and into a narrow alley.

"Pheb!" I heard Addison yelling from the phone.

I put the phone back up to my ear and started walking towards the street. "I'm sorry. I'm back now."

"How did you end up in bed with a stripper?"

"What?!" I heard Daphne yelling in the background.

"I don't know. What happened last night? And why in God's name would you let me leave with a stripper?"

"I didn't!"

"God, why is this happening to me?"

"Pheb, what all do you remember about last night?"

"Shit! Not too much. We got dressed, headed for Caesars, and that's really about it. No! Wait, I remember Gray Mercy."

"God, you drank Old Gray Mere? No wonder you can't remember shit," Addison snickered.

"What's Old Gray Mere?"

"A little bit of shit and hell in a cup."

"Where is she?" I heard Daphne again.

"She doesn't know yet."

I stepped out towards the front of the building and looked up. "I'm at the Venetian."

"Oh honey. Hail a cab. You don't know how to get back to the hotel."

I flagged down a cab and hung up with Addison.

By the time I got back to the hotel, I had to do the ultimate walk of shame. I felt everyone's eyes on me, and my stomach turned. I slid my key card into the slot, and the light turned green. I walked in, not making eye contact with any of them. The main sitting room was trashed. They must've had a wild night. The room looked like it had been hit by a tornado. Clothes, shoes, and empty champagne bottles were thrown all over the place. I just walked by them all and headed for my bathroom.

"Honey, wait!" I heard Addison calling for me, but as I passed, I threw one hand up and kept walking.

I knew I would cry in the shower, but I wasn't prepared to do this in front of an audience. I got to the bathroom, shut the door, and turned on the water. I removed my earrings and slid off my bracelet. I took off both of my rings and heard a gentle knock at the door.

Wait a second; I usually only wore one ring, not two. I definitely should not have had a princess-cut, diamond ring on my left hand. I picked the sparkly ring up and stared at it with wide eyes.

There was another light knock at the door again.

"Who is it?" I asked while still in a daze.

"Your husband," a rough unfamiliar voice said to me.

I looked over at the door as it opened slowly and there stood the stripper. He held a key in his hand and gave me a small grin. I remembered when we checked in, the bellboy told us that each bedroom had a key in the kitchen draw.

He said, "People get locked out or they lock themselves in their own rooms. This is Vegas." He winked back at us when he showed us the keys.

One of the girls must have given the spare to him. Them coldblooded Bitches.

CHAPTER 1

The Groom

Xavier James Luther was thirty-two years old. He didn't have any children and had never been married. He was from Hugo, Oklahoma, but now lived in Mountain Ranch, California. I had heard of Calaveras County before, but I always thought it was nothing but wild cattle up there. He had two Labradors, eighteen chickens, one rooster, six guineas, one hundred cows, forty sheep, seven horses, four donkeys, six bulls, and twenty-two pigs. He told me all this at the edge of my hotel bed.

Xavier was extremely handsome, but I wasn't letting that clog my mind. He was obvious slow of some sort or maybe he had a mental issue. I was shit-faced drunk last night, but he had told me twice already that he remembered everything that happened perfectly. So, he was obviously sober and he obviously wanted this marriage to stay active.

"I don't have any money," I told him quickly before he could tell me something else about him.

"Why are you telling me this?"

"Because you should know. I make 54 K a year, and Sallie Mae student loans are kicking my ass. I'm a couple of paychecks from being broke. This trip alone has taken my checking account down to its last nine hundred dollars. My rent is $1,800 a month, my car note is $600 a month, my car insurance is $150 a month, and I have illegal cable. I steal my downstairs neighbor's Wi-Fi, and I sometimes steal my neighbor's Sunday paper from across the hall . . . while he's at church. I'm a very bad person, and I can barely take care of myself."

I was hoping that would've woken him up from his slumber. He was probably thinking since I was a hefty girl that I could cook, well that was a negative. He probably found out what I did for a living, but life as a paralegal was not what it was all cracked up to be. On the other hand, he might have thought I had childbearing hips and maybe he wanted a couple of kids pushed out of me.

He chuckled and stood. "I know you don't remember any of this, but I told you last night, I love you and you only. I wanted to marry you, Phoebe Alexis Courtland."

Oh shit, he knew my government name.

"You gotta go," I uttered immediately.

"Wait, what?"

"Leave! You! Now!"

"Phebs?"

"I'm sorry. I don't know you," I said as I pushed him out of the room.

He didn't fight me on this but just backed away with his palms up. I slammed the door in his face and then locked it.

I stripped down and finally got into the shower. I tried to scrub everything off me. I wish I could've cleared my head up a bit so I could remember everything that had happened last night. When the water turned ice cold, I got out of the tub. I dressed in t-shirt and jeans; I had no energy to put on anything else. I cracked the door and saw the girls sitting on the couches.

I pushed out a big breath and opened the door wide. "Thank God! He finally left."

They all looked at me with wide eyes, and then Addison pointed behind me. I turned and there stood Xavier, drinking a glass of milk. He gave me a wave. I turned around and went back into my bedroom, closing the door. This went on into the wee hours of the night. Everyone tried to get me out of my room… well, everyone but him. I never heard another peep from him for the rest of the evening. I finally couldn't take it anymore. I slid into some flats and grabbed my wallet to go out to search for food. I walked out into the sitting area; there wasn't a soul insight. I guessed everyone had gone to bed, and the rancher finally gave up. I opened the front door quietly and gently pulled it shut. I turned around, and he stood.

"Phebs please don't run from me."

I walked past him and headed for the elevators. He followed behind me silently. Neither one of us said a word. We, both, got onto the elevator and rode it down. The bell dinged and the door opened once we got to the bottom floor. A wedding party was waiting to get on, and it sickened me to my stomach. I rolled my eyes and stomped past the kissing couple, who couldn't keep their hands off each other. We passed by the front desk, and the friendly concierge smiled wide. He snapped his fingers at a small group of employees, and they rushed towards a luggage holder loaded with flowers. Each one of them picked up an arrangement of some sort.

"Señor, I have the bouquets," he called out to Xavier.

Xavier didn't say a word, and he didn't lose his stride behind me. The employees all smiled wide at Xavier and frowned once he past them with their arrangements in hand.

"Señor!" the concierge yelled.

We walked out the front entrance and headed for the strip. He stayed behind me and never said a word. After a couple of blocks, I felt a light tug at my elbow. I turned and Xavier was holding a door wide for me at one of the strip's diners. It was called Vicky's Diner, and it had an old school greasy spoon diner feel. There were Tiffany styled lamps everywhere. It made me smile and think of my grandmother's sitting room. She loved Tiffany style lamps, and I had two of her favorites in my apartment.

I walked in, and Xavier followed behind me. I was admiring the lamps when he lightly tugged at my arm again. He walked down to the last booth, and I followed. He waited until I sat down before he had his seat; he acted like the perfect gentleman.

"Hi, you two. Oh, you know what they say. Once you last your first twenty-four hours in Vegas, you'll be together forever." The waitress wore a wide smile.

"Honey Dew, you want the French toast again?" she asked.

I nodded.

"And Cowboy, you want the steak and eggs, right?"

"Yes, Ma'am," Xavier said to the red-lipped waitress.

"Oh and I gave your card and book to my boss a couple of hours ago. We'll see what he says," she whispered over to him.

He grinned and nodded while she walked away to place our orders.

"So, is this some kind of twisted version of *Hangover*?"

"What do you mean?" he moved in and whispered across the booth from me. I could tell he wanted me to talk a little softer. He stared around with a small grin at the people staring at us.

"I mean this." I waved my hand in the air, still putting on a show for the patrons. "Apparently, we came here last night." I crossed my arms and squeezed myself tight.

"Phoebe, the last thing I wanted to do was upset you."

"Well, it didn't work," I said forcefully to him.

Our waitress came back with two waters and two coffees. I picked up the coffee at once, but I shook so hard that most of it was on the table. I was in a state of rage and trying to focus on one thing right now was almost impossible. He yanked some napkins out of the dispenser and started wiping up my mess at once.

"Kit, can we get Phebs a glass of O.J.? She hasn't eaten anything all day, and I think her stomach would appreciate a little sugar first."

"Oh, sure thing." She touched my shoulder gently and walked back towards the counter.

"Do you want to leave? Is this place upsetting you too much?"

"No! I want you to leave because you're upsetting me too much!"

He put his head down and shook it from side to side. "I won't leave you."

For some reason, his words meant so much more than if he just walked out the door without saying anything. I felt safe with him, and I didn't know why. I wanted to reach over and place my hand in his. I imaged he would kiss it and rub it against his face. I could almost feel the stubble from his chin on my hands. I watched his face now, and I could tell he imagined the same thing. I edged my hand towards him, and he slowly reached for me.

"Here's your O.J., Honey Dew," the waitress interrupted us.

I shot my hand back into my lap, but Xavier's lingered on the table. He watched me with desperate eyes. I had a strong feeling this man would wait forever for me. I gave the waitress a small smile and she went to the table next to us.

"Give me your hand?" he begged in a whisper.

His whisper made my insides moan. I shifted in my seat.

"Phoebe?" he whispered again.

I closed my eyes, clenched my now pulsating vagina, and whispered, "No."

"Look at me, Phebs?"

"No, X," and then my eyes shot wide open. I looked at him, and he was grinning from ear to ear.

"You called me X!" His eyes lit up like Christmas.

"You haven't called me that since . . . " He drifted off a little, and I saw whatever he was thinking made his eyes roll to the back of his head. "Well, you haven't called me that in a while." He had a little more pep in him now, and he shifted in his seat as if he couldn't stay still.

"How did we meet?" I asked him.

"We... we met here," he choked.

"Here?"

"We met right here in this booth. Addison dared you to come over and ask me if I had a farm... And I told you yes. Then, you rolled your eyes and sat down. Then, you asked me if I had a horse. I told you yes, and you took your jacket off. Then, you asked me if I had a tractor, and I told you yes. You pulled off one of your earrings, then. . ."

"Strip date," I breathed.

"Yeah, that's what you called it."

"You must have looked very cowboyish last night."

"Well, yes, ma'am, I did, Wranglers and all."

"You don't look very cowboyish tonight."

"No, no I don't. I had to run for my life to catch my wife this morning, so I left the Wranglers at my hotel." Xavier looked down at the table. He pushed his wedding band around and around his ring finger now.

19

Kit came back with our spread. Xavier held his head down for grace and then started eating. This man ate as if he was starving.

"Have you not eaten today?"

"No ma'am. If you don't eat, then I don't eat."

I rolled my eyes and he laughed at me.

"So, what do you know about me?"

"Don't you want to know how far you got with the strip date?" he asked.

"No need."

"Why not?"

"Because you're not the kind of guy that would let a girl go that far in public."

"I wouldn't."

"I figured."

He stared at me for a moment and then cleared his throat. "Well, you've been a paralegal for almost seven years. You have a white Persian named Meow Meow. You drive an Infinite. You're terrified of horses, you can't swim, you're an only child, and you're from LA. Your parents were never married, you're not religious, and your left foot is a half a size bigger than your right. Your favorite color is red, your birthday is August the 5th, you hate gladiator sandals, and you love spinach and Brussels Sprouts. You want to own your own clothing store for the not so perfect bodies. You wish you had a big family, but you, your mom, and dad are all from one-child families. You and Addison have been best friends since pre-k, and you and Daphne met in junior high."

I stared at him. This man knew my life story, and I don't even remember telling him.

"And, you have a birthmark on your right inner thigh; it's kind of shaped like Ivy," he whispered over to me.

I dropped my fork. I couldn't eat another bite. He had really messed me up big time. A man came over to our table and asked Xavier if he had time to speak with him now. He nodded, wiped his mouth, and slid over in the booth. The man sat down next to him, right across from me.

"Honey, this will take just a second," he said to me.

I gave him a smile and waved them to go ahead.

"Mr. Gaines, this is my beautiful wife, Phoebe. Phoebe, this is Mr. Gaines. He is one of the managers of this fine establishment."

Gaines pushed his hand out for me, and I shook it. Then, he sat down a thin folder and opened it.

Xavier poured ketchup on his hash browns and drizzled hot sauce on top. "Honey, try these. You love them like this."

He pushed his plate towards me, reached over, and took mine. He dived straight in as if it was his plate. I took a fork full of the bloody looking hash browns. I closed my eyes and sucked in all the many flavors. The hash browns were amazing; I opened my eyes and noticed I had an audience. Both of the men sitting across from me stared. Mr. Gaines was blushing, and Xavier's breathing was slow and long. I gave them a smile and dug in for some more. The men were done by the time I had finished everything on Xavier's plate. They shook hands, and Xavier laid two twenties on the table.

"Are you ready?" he asked me with a hand for me to take.

I nodded but refused to take his hand. He held the door open for me. I went out back to the strip. I turned back towards the hotel, and Xavier cleared his throat.

"If you wouldn't mind, I would like to take you back through last night. Maybe your memory will kick in."

"Where did we go after this?"

"You said I had to ask you on a real date, so I did."

"Where did we go?"

22

"I'll take you there." He reached his hand out for me.

"No!" I growled.

"Phoebe, this may trigger the memories back. I think we should do everything just like we did last night."

I glared at him before snatching his hand. "And no funny business."

"I wouldn't dare try any funny business with my legally bonded wife."

"Don't be a smart-ass."

He grinned at me. When he saw my killer stare, he coughed out a laugh. We held hands down the strip, and we looked stupid with so many people "awhhhing" and "oh how sweeting" us. We finally made it to a theater, and he purchased two tickets for the special feature. We walked in and went right past the concession stand. We got our seat right in the center of the theater.

"What are we watching?"

"Shhhh, it's a surprise," he said while he hushed me.

I grinded my teeth together. He was truly getting on my nerves, and I was seconds away from getting up and leaving his ass there. The lights dimmed and the movie started. When I saw the title and the names running across the scene, I froze.

"A Patch of Blue? That's my absolute favorite Sidney Poitier movie."

"Yes, so I've heard."

I sunk deeper into my seat and Xavier put his arms around me. I elbowed him.

He doubled over with his hands up in the air. "Sorry," he whispered.

I crossed my arms tight and crossed my legs away from him.

A Patch of Blue was a movie made in the mid 60's. It was about a blind, white, uneducated girl who was befriended by a black man. The black man becomes determined to help her escape her impoverished and very abusive home life. Of course, they fall in love at the end, and in the 60's a black man and a white woman was still a forbidden. By the end of the movie, I was a blubbering fool. Xavier handed me a few napkins from the café. I took them and used them at once.

"I didn't have any last night, and I knew if you let me bring you again, you would probably need them."

I smiled at him and then I kissed him on his lips. I don't know what came over me; I was caught up in the moment. I pulled away from him and he glared at me like he wanted to attack me. His eyes were hungry. He pulled me back to him, and he placed his lips on mine. His kiss was urgent but still sweet. He held me by the back of my neck, and I couldn't move from him. He kissed like a pro, and I couldn't get any clear thoughts in my head.

"Phoebe, if you would just give me tonight. I swear that I'm yours, and I will show you that I'm the right one," he whispered that deep whisper in my ear.

I was lost in his words, and I was mad at myself for letting myself get this caught up. My heart had been trampled on so many times. And, at least, those other times were by people I knew. Xavier was a complete stranger. I pushed him away and got up from my chair. I stomped out the theater and then we were back on the strip. Xavier looked pissed. He held his arm out for me to go left of the theater. I stomped passed him and walked on down the strip. I turned around a couple of times to make sure he was still there.

"I'm not going to leave you," he told me, and once again, his meaning meant so much more to me than the words.

I slowed as he came up beside me. I placed my arm through his. I didn't want to hear anything else from the passers-by if they saw us holding hands again. An arm through someone else was innocent and no one would be the wiser. Friends or Lovers? People didn't care as much, but handholding was some serious shit. There was a small carnival in a field ahead and I felt my heart skip a few beats. I loved circuses and carnivals just like a kid did.

"Xavier, was the carnival here last night?"

"Yes," he said a little softer to me now.

"Did we go?"

"Yes, but not until later."

"Oh, can we go now?"

"I think we should wait until later."

"Please, I really want to go now."

He watched my face and then he caved. "Okay," he said with a small smile. I grinned from ear to ear. "I hope they have the rainbow cotton candy."

"They do."

I looked over at him, giggled, and laid my head on his arm. He kissed the top of my head. Xavier paid our admission and I was searching for the cotton candy. "It's over here." He pointed.

I smiled and followed him. He held his hand out for me, and I took it into mine. We got to the window. The lady smiled at us.

"A rainbow cotton candy and a lemonade, please," Xavier told her.

I looked over at him because that's exactly what I would have ordered.

The lady smiled and went to get our order.

"I want to ride the Ferris wheel," I proclaimed.

"Later," he said reaching for his lemonade. He sat the straw right in front of me.

"I'll get some after my cotton candy."

"It won't be as sweet after then."

I thought about it and took a swig; it was delish. I handed it back to him, and he drank some. He handed me my cotton candy and I dove in. After my third bite, I noticed he was watching me.

"Oh, do you want some?" I asked with a mouth full of pillow-soft sugar.

He laughed. "No, I never really liked cotton candy."

"What?"

"I know. It's strange, right?"

I set a piece of cotton candy on my lips and then summoned him with my pointing finger. I made the come here movement very slowly. He grinned wide and walked over to me. He licked the cotton candy off my lips first, and then he pressed his lips on mine. Our tongues played tug of war for minute or two. We heard the howling calls, so I pushed him away from me. I laughed at the guys howling behind us; I bent over and bowed down to them. I turned around to face Xavier, and he had a serious look on his face.

"What's wrong?" I asked him.

He pulled me back to him and kissed me softly and sweet this time. I was all wrapped up in him that I didn't see myself releasing him anytime soon. Xavier pulled back a little but still kept me in his embrace.

"Hey, let's go," I whispered.

His face dropped a little, and I didn't understand why.

"No, Phebs."

"Why not?"

Xavier frowned and untwisted our arms and bodies from each other. He started walking deeper into the carnival. I followed behind him. He slowed down at a set of bleachers. He sat down and watched the horse show that was already in session. I sat right next to him while he kept his eyes on the horses.

"Do you like horses?" I quizzed.

"Yes, I told you all this last night." Xavier was obviously annoyed with me.

"Listen, I'm sorry, and I really gave it my all, but we're both two different people. And, this is obviously not working for either of us."

"What?" he snapped back at me a little too loudly.

I turned back around and faced the field with the horses. Xavier got up from his seat and walked back the way we came.

I sat there for a while and walked towards the restroom. Once I was done, I looked for him a little bit, but I never saw him. I walked past a series of tents. I started getting a little nervous. I left my phone in my room, and I wasn't hundred percent sure where I was. I prepared myself to start hoofing it when I saw him at the front entrance. I walked up to him, and he wouldn't look at me.

"Are you ready to go?" I asked.

"I thought you wanted to ride the Ferris wheel."

"Nah, I changed my mind," I said with a breath.

We walked back to my hotel, neither one of us said a word to each other. Every now and then, we would pass by an establishment, and he would look at me, but I didn't remember anything from last night. Watching him grasp for these invisible straws was starting to crush me. When we got to my hotel, he was getting ready to walk in with me.

"Xavier, I'm sorry I don't remember you, but my lawyer will contact yours next week. We need to take care of this immediately. I hope you understand."

He didn't say anything as he just looked at me.

"Hey, you seem like a really good guy, and I'm not really sure why you're single, but any girl up to your standards would be a complete fool to let you go. I'm really not sure what you were expecting to get from me, but I'm not your Mrs. Right. I'm not anybody's Mrs. Anything. I'm sorry." I walked up to him and gave him a kiss on his cheek. I turned, but he grabbed my elbow, stopping me from walking away from him.

"I love you," Xavier told me like his life depended on it.

I pulled away from his grip and stepped into the hotel lobby. When I got to the room, everyone was still soundly sleeping. I looked at the clock; it was 4:30 in the morning. Our flight was leaving at two that afternoon, so I had time to catch up on some sleep. I emailed James and told him I needed him to write up some divorce papers. I told him Xavier's full name and that I would explain later. I laid down on the bed, and the last thing I saw before I went to sleep was the princess cut ring.

CHAPTER 2

The Divorce

"My favorite color is red. What's yours?" I asked.

"Light brown."

"Light brown? Who says that?"

"I like the color of Hay. I have a field on the side of my house that's full of haystacks and I like to look at it."

"Hay is a tan/beige/yellowish color."

"Yeah… but, I think you're beautiful and I can look at you every day instead of the hay."

"Screw the hay," I blurted out with a fist in the air.

Xavier laughed and pulled me close to him. "Yeah, screw the hay."

He kissed me. It was the softest, sweetest kiss ever. The lights from the Ferris wheel were almost like magic. They twinkled and danced all around us.

"I love you," left my lips, and I heard my own heart stop.

"I fell in love with you three hours ago. You're late," he told me with a grin. My heart kick-started itself back to life.

"Marry me, Phoebe."

"Anytime and any place. I've been waiting for you to ask me that for like three hours. You're late." He laughed and kissed me again.

The Ferris wheel stopped, and we got off.

"Come on! Let's go get you the biggest and baddest ring."

We ran out of the carnival laughing, excited, and in love.

I woke up with a jerk. I turned and he wasn't there.

"X!" I called out for him, but he didn't answer. "Xavier!" I yelled from the bed, but still nothing.

I jumped up and went searching for him. He wasn't in the bathroom, and I started to panic.

"Honey, what's wrong?" Addison asked me through a yawn.

"Where's Xavier?"

"Honey, last time I saw him, he was sitting outside in the hallway."

I slid my flats on and went to the front door. I swung it wide, but no one was there.

"Oh God!" I panicked.

"Calm down and breathe. When was the last time you saw him?"

"God!"

"What is it, Phebs?"

"He's gone!"

"Stop it. He would never leave you and you know that."

"No, Addi. I was horrible to him last night. I was a monster to him. I didn't remember, but I do remember. I remember everything. Oh God, Addi. He's gone!"

"Call him."

I reached for my phone. "Shit, it's dead." I ran over to the charger and plugged the phone in.

"Call his hotel room," Daphne said, wearing her Care Bears pajama pants and white t-shirt.

I ran over to the phone on the table. "Where was he staying?"

Both of them gave me a blank stare.

"Wait, um, got it! He was staying at the Venetian." I opened the phone book and found the number.

"Thank you for choosing the Venetian, home of the --"

"Sorry," I cut off the woman at the front desk. "I need to locate my husband before he checks out of the hotel."

"What's the room number?"

"I don't know. His name is Xavier James Luther and I am Mrs. Luther."

"I'm sorry, Mrs. Luther, but we have to have a room number."

I thought about that. "Hand me my purse!" I pointed to my room.

Daphne ran over and set it down in front of me. I fumbled through it and found the piece of paper. It was a bill from X's hotel.

"R-13."

"Oh, that's one of our Renaissance suites, and it's an excellent choice."

"Come on, man," I whined.

"I'm sorry, Madam, but the party has already checked out of that room."

"When?"

"Three hours ago. Did you need to reserve it for a special occasion? We have excellent rates –"

I hung the phone up and just sat there.

"Honey, we'll find him," Addison assured me.

"He's gone, Addi. He's gone."

**

We showered, packed up, and dressed. No one said a word. We all piled up in the cab and headed for the airport. I stared out the window and just let the tears fall where they may. I didn't care who heard me or who saw me.

"Stop the car, stop the car!" I shouted.

The cab driver pulled over and stopped at the curb. I jumped out of the car and ran for the front door. Smelling the greasy food gave me so many memories now. The way he looked, laughed and smelt. I had to push my emotions way down. I had a mission for this diner visit.

"Have a seat, sweetheart. Someone will be with you in a moment," the waitress passing by said to me.

"Is Kit here?"

"Who's asking?"

"I was one of her customers from last night and I really need to talk to her."

"No, she got off at five."

"Is Mr. Gaines here?"

"No, he won't be back until Tuesday."

"My husband gave Mr. Gaines a folder of his farm business, and Mr. Gaines was considering using his services."

"What kind of service?"

"Produce and milk," I replied.

"Well, ain't that bout a bitch."

"I'm sorry?"

"My nephew is his produce guy, sweetheart."

"Sir, all I need is a number. I think he gave him one in that folder. He may have left it here, on his desk maybe?"

"Sweetheart, you better get out of here before I get Little T to kick your pretty little teeth in."

I looked over at Little T, and she wasn't nothing I wanted to wrestle with. She was at least six feet tall and had shoulders like a linebacker and the body of a bear. I turned around and walked out of the café.

When I got back to the car, I started wailing. By the time we landed at SFO, I wasn't talking to anyone. We got into Daphne's car, and I was dropped off first. I unlocked my door, dragged my suitcase inside, and collapsed on the floor.

A couple of hours later, I decided to try to search for him myself. Xavier James Luther did not have a website, he did not have a landline in his name, and he had no social media accounts. It was like he was a ghost. Maybe he was putting on a scam. No, he couldn't have been. He gave Mr. Gaines that folder with all the farm information in it.

Dammit, why couldn't I remember the name of his farm?

My cell phone rang and I bolted for it. The screen said James and I sighed.

James had been my boss for six years and he had been my Godfather all my life. He and my father went to law school together, and they were the best of buds. James didn't have any children of his own, but he'd always been a second father to me.

I wished this were Xavier James calling me.

"Hello, James."

"Married, Phoebe? And in Vegas? You sound like a tourist."

"I know, I know. It's a long story."

"I will see you in the morning, young lady. We have a debriefing and then, it's you and I. Did I make myself clear?"

"Yes, sir, and James, don't tell Dad."

James grunted and disconnected the line.

I swallowed hard as I sat there in a slump for a long while. I ordered Chinese takeout, watched a couple of re-runs, and went to bed.

I knocked on James' door the next morning. I breathed in and out until I heard him say, "Come in."

James sat behind his desk with his glasses at the tip of his nose. He was the same age as my father, but he didn't look anywhere near it. He said having children aged people and that's why he never had children. But, my mom said differently. She said that James had a girlfriend he wanted to marry. She said James liked things to be in a certain order, his girlfriend was a free spirit, and that things just didn't work out between them.

"Have a seat, Phoebe," he ordered.

38

I sat down, dreading this conversation. I knew James was disappointed in me and that made this even worse.

He pulled his glasses off and leaned back in his chair. "So what happened?"

"I went to the conference and --"

"No!" he interrupted me.

"I met him at a café."

"Which café?"

"Vicky's Café."

James made a few notes and that made me feel even worse. He was treating me like a client and not like his goddaughter. "And?"

"We talked and talked, walked and walked, and then it just happened."

"I understand that tourists go to Vegas, fall miraculously in love, and get married. But Phoebe, you go to Vegas all the time, and you decided to marry some cowboy from the sticks?"

"Uncle James, you found him?"

"Of course I found him. Who do you think I am?"

"I need to see him."

"Oh, and you will. You will be driving down there tomorrow morning and I don't give a damn how long it takes you. He will sign these god-dammed papers. You do whatever the hell you have to do. No, Godniece of mine is marrying a hillbilly."

"But Uncle James --"

"Shut up. I don't want to hear shit else from you. This did not happen, and I can get it sponged clean. This marriage cannot last longer than thirty days. Do you understand me?"

I sat there for a minute. This did not go as I planned. I didn't want to divorce Xavier, but I knew my uncle was right. This was not a good look for me right now. I was taking the bar in forty-five days, and I really didn't need these distractions.

"Phoebe, this is a business trip, so use the company car and your company credit card. Caress will give you your itinerary. I want this to look as professional as possible."

"Yes, sir."

"Leave at noon today so you can pack and get some rest."

"Yes, sir." I stood.

"Phoebe, don't come back here until those papers are all signed. I don't want to hear from you until then."

"Yes, sir." I walked out of his office with tears welling up in my eyes. I walked a little too fast towards the bathroom.

"Phoebe, I have your itinerary!" Caress called after me.

Everyone watched, and I held it together until I got to the bathroom. Once I was in there, I lost it.

A few minutes later, there was a knock on the stall. I stopped crying at once.

"Phoebe, are you alright, Honey?" It was Caress at the door.

"I'm fine, Caress. I'm just not feeling well. I'm about to leave for the day."

"Honey, come out so I can take a look at you."

I blew my nose and flushed the toilet. I opened the stall, and Caress stood there with open arms. I walked right into them; I couldn't help it. Caress was about ten years older than I was and her name said it all. She was the gentlest person I knew. She had been working as James' assistant for thirteen years.

"There now. You pull yourself together before you go out with the wolves."

"I will," I hiccupped.

"Now, you listen to me. Don't you dare let a man make a woman's decision? You do whatever you want and feel you need to do."

Great! Just great. Caress thought I was pregnant.

"I'm not pregnant, Caress."

"Well, Honey, there's only one or two things that could have you this upset. And you just came back from your trip to Vegas and --" She broke off.

I stared at her in silence.

"Phoebe, you didn't!"

I turned from her.

"Honey, is it that cowboy up in Calaveras County? James had me searching for that man all night. I thought he was some kind of underground cock or dog fighter."

"No, just my husband." I sighed.

"Oh, Honey, he seems like a real nice guy." I just stared at her. "Oh, James doesn't approve of him?"

"I have to go, Caress."

"Phoebe, if you love him and if you want to be with him, then let it be. This is your decision, not anybody else's."

I gave her a hug and headed out of the bathroom. I packed my briefcase and laptop. I had to make this look as professional as possible. I knew Caress would keep her mouth shut; she had to for thirteen years. I was sure she had seen and done things I didn't want to hear anything about.

I called Addison's phone and it went straight to voicemail. I told her that I would be out of town for a couple of weeks before I went home and packed. By the time I was done, it was a little after one. I decided to go ahead and take the drive out to Calaveras County. It took me two and half hours to get there and the drive was beautiful. Caress had gotten me a room at one the local resorts, a five-star establishment.

When I pulled in, I noticed right away the ratings for this place had to have been a couple of stars at the least. It looked a little wild, weeds were unruly and, there were only three cars in the giant parking lot. I dragged my bags to the front door and had to rest before I continued.

An elderly man came out to help me. "Welcome to the Calaveras County Five Star Resort."

"Hello."

"You must be the lawyer."

"Well, um, yes sir."

"Ah, now, none of that 'sir' business. I'm Ben, and here's my lovely wife, Pauline."

"It's very nice to meet you both," I said with a smile.

"Now, Sugar, the lady on the phone didn't tell us how long you'd be staying," she said with a smile.

I wondered if there was a convention coming to town because there wasn't anybody here.

"Maybe a week or two. Is that alright?"

"Oh yes, Sugar. We just like to know, that's all. Benji! Benji!" she yelled.

A pimple-faced teenager came from around the corner, texting.

"Take Mrs. . . ." She dragged the Mrs. part out because she didn't know what my last name was.

"Ms. Courtland," I quickly answered.

"Take Ms. Courtland's bags up to her room."

Benji reached around and threw the bags on a luggage carrier.

"Blessed be, Benji. Be careful with those, and where's your hat?"

The teen pulled a round hat from his back pocket. It was all crumpled and smashed.

"Well," Pauline breathed out in a huff.

I signed the three forms and went up to my room. There were only three floors there and I was on the top. Benji was standing outside my room when I got there.

He never lifted his eyes from his phone as he said, "Here's the bathroom, kitchen area, bedroom's in there, and here's your sitting room. Have a nice stay." He walked out of the room.

I held a bill out for him, but he was too busy texting to notice.

"Benji?" I called after him.

"Yes, ma'am?" He finally looked up and saw the twenty-dollar bill dangling in his face. His eyes got wide, and he gave me a huge smile. He had the biggest braces I'd ever seen. And, good grief he had horse teeth. I prayed those braces helped with that mouth of his.

"Thank you, Ms. Courtland and if you need anything else, just call down to the front desk." Benji left, staring at the twenty all the way down the hall.

I changed clothes and decided to go ahead and try to find Xavier's farm. I put on a t-shirt and jeans with a pair of rain boots. I had a feeling I would be knee deep in something squishy or liquid like. I went down to the front desk, and Ben was behind the counter now.

"Excuse me, Ben. I'm trying to find Xavier Luther's farm."

"Well," he laughed. I watched him carefully. "Let me show you." He walked outside and I followed. He went around to the back of the resort; we walked along the deck. He pointed in the distance "There's Xavier's place... All of that... and there... and even there."

It was ginormous and I wasn't prepared for all of this.

"You really don't need to drive that little car down there. How about I give you a lift and you just call me when you're ready to come on back?"

I nodded with a smile.

We got in Ben's pickup and bounced all the way to Xavier's place. It took us about fifteen minutes, and I couldn't see a thing but trees until we pulled up to the front gates. They were massive and looked like they were guarding the grounds. I'm sure these trees were planted years ago and not placed here a year or two ago. The gates had to be ten feet tall all the way around. Ben pushed the buzzer and someone spoke through the box.

"Is he expecting you?" Ben asked me in a whisper.

I shook my head.

"Now, you ain't coming up here to start no trouble with Xavier, are you?"

I shook my head no again, but this time with a frown.

"Alright then," he gave me a warning tone.

"It's Ben Cumberland, and I have a delivery for Xavier."

"Come on in, Ben," the voice from the box greeted him.

The gates unlocked and sounded like it unlocked some more before they started opening slowly. Once they opened wide enough for the pickup to fit through, Ben drove on in.

We drove down a long driveway and I saw the house. Well, "house" was an understatement. It was more like a compound, big as it was. Two big droopy looking dogs came running up to the Pickup. Ben stopped the truck and shut the engine off.

"Hey there, Sonic, and hey there, Boom." Ben greeted both dogs.

They jumped up on Ben, and he patted and rubbed at them.

I put my satchel across me and jumped out of the truck. The one he called Sonic came over and sniffed at me then dropped down to the ground.

"Oh my God!!! What's wrong with him?" I asked Ben frantically.

"Ah, he's just flirting with you. Get up from there, Sonic."

The dog jumped straight up. He kept sniffing me, but he never jumped on me, thank God.

We walked around to the back of the ranch and then I got the full effect. There was a pond, two barns, a few sheds, horse stables and then fields and fields of animals everywhere. There were all segregated, but there were hundreds of them. I saw a few little houses out in the distance, but it was obvious they belonged to the massive property. There were so many people walking around working. They acted as if it was nine o'clock in the morning. I leaned against one of the huge beams just trying to soak it all in.

"Ben! What you been up to? Clara said you had a delivery for me."

I heard Xavier's voice coming from the side of us.

"Hey, Xavier. Nothing much, just trying to take in as much fishing as I can. And yes, I do have a delivery for you."

I cringed behind the beam, sweating bullets now.

"Well, where is it?"

"She *was* right here."

"Well, hell, who is it?"

"It's your wife," I told him, stepping from around the beam.

Everything on that farm got very still and very quiet. Ben's eyes were wide as dinner plates, and the rest of the nearby crew was frozen by my words.

"Goddammit," Xavier spit through his teeth. "God dammit!" he said a little bit louder now.

"Now, you looked at me straight in the eyes and you said you weren't coming to bring any trouble," Ben scolded me.

"Don't worry, Ben. She fooled me, too. You just go on ahead and take her right on back with you. She's not wanted or welcomed here." He turned from us and started walking in the opposite direction.

I opened my satchel and yanked the papers out. "Xavier, just sign these papers and you'll never have to see me again!" I yelled out to him.

He didn't stop. I ran after him and all the workers moved out of my way. The men tipped their hats at me, and the women all nodded. He stomped into the horse stables while three men followed him. They all wore the same style gear. Wranglers, huge belt buckles, and plaid or solid shirts. Oh and they wore boots. All I could see were boots and more boots.

"Xavier!"

He still didn't slow. He went into a stall and I tucked my jeans into my boots.

"Just sign the damn papers, and I'll leave you alone," I yelled over the stall at him.

The three men in the barn snickered at me.

I jumped up and down, trying to get some kind of reaction to him. He acted as if I wasn't even standing there.

"Just give me the damn divorce."

He walked out of the stall and then I shoved the papers in his face. He never once looked at me. He walked into another stall. I held the papers over the stall, but he wouldn't take them.

The men were still laughing at me and it was pissing me off. I growled as I pulled the papers back from over the stall. I dropped the papers in a pile of what I prayed was not manure. I screamed at the top of my lungs, bent over through one of the gaps in the fence to get the papers, and there was a loud thud.

Xavier yelled my name and then everything went dark.

CHAPTER 3

The Bride

Once again, my head was swimming and I could not latch on to my surroundings. I felt a soft bed under me, and there were at least six, maybe seven, pillows. I reached out to both of sides, not knowing what I was reaching for. I opened my eyes, but there was nothing but darkness. I didn't see a strip of light anywhere. I'd gone blind.

I remembered that I had been in the stables arguing with Xavier, and there was a loud thud. My head was throbbing, but now I was blind, and I didn't know where I was. I started screaming and crying. I yelled and screamed some more, and nothing. *Where was I?*

"Help me! Please! Help me!" I looked around and around, and nothing came to view.

"Phoebe," I heard Xavier yelling for me.

I heard someone running towards me. I screamed even louder. I heard a thump at the door, and then the room was filled with lights. There were lights in the ceiling, coming from the walls, and at both sides of the California king bed I was on.

Xavier ran over to me and jumped in the bed with me, pulling me up against him.

"What's wrong? Are you hurt?"

"I thought I was blind," I cried out into his chest.

"What?"

"I couldn't see anything. There was no light. I couldn't see."

"I'm sorry, baby. I didn't leave a light on for you. I didn't think about what would happen if you woke up and I wasn't here."

"You left me," I whimpered into his chest

"What?"

"You said you wouldn't leave me, but you left me."

"Guys, I think she's okay. Give us a minute."

I turned around and saw five people standing in the bedroom. I started crying some more, now out of pure embarrassment. Everyone left the room; it was time for Mr. and Mrs. to have a heart to heart.

"Now, what are you talking about?" Xavier questioned.

"I woke up that next morning and I remembered everything."

He didn't move. I squeezed him a little tighter, but I didn't even think he noticed. Xavier was in a daze now and I had put him there.

"I called your hotel, but they said you had checked out. Then, I went back to the Vicky's Café just to see if Mr. Gaines had your number or the name of your farm, but he wasn't there."

Xavier reached over to the nightstand closest to him, and he put something in my hand. It was my cell phone.

"Go to the H's."

I obeyed and when I made it to the H's, he tapped the screen and scrolled down. The name he stopped on was "Hubby".

I shook my head, pulled my legs up, and wrapped my arms around them. I could have called him all this time, but I didn't know. We both sat there for a long while, not saying anything to one another.

He finally broke the silence. "Since you came here yesterday and paraded around the fact that we were married, I need you to stay until Sunday."

"Why?"

"Because my entire family is coming today."

"Why?"

He slid away from me and lifted me from the bed.

"They're all coming to meet the bride," he told me walking out the door.

"X."

"Don't call me that."

"I'm sorry. My clothes are up at the resort."

"I went and got them yesterday. And, Clara grabbed you a few things from town; they're all in your armoire." He walked out the door and shut it behind him.

I got up and found I was stiff all over. I stretched and that did not help. I almost had to hobble over to the armoire. I opened it and frowned. Everything in there was country western type clothes. I did perk up when I saw there were two pairs of boots sitting by the armoire, a brown pair, and a black pair. These were my very first real pair of cowgirl boots.

I showered and dressed. I wore a pair of dark wranglers, a pink tank top, and a plaid pink and black button down. I pulled on my black boots and pulled all my hair up in a ponytail. I looked the part one hundred percent. I looked in the closet, and it was completely empty. I checked all of the drawers, and they were completely empty as well. There was a knock at the door. I went to go answer it.

An older Hispanic woman stood there. "Good morning, Mrs. Luther, I am Clara, Mr. Luther's head house assistant." She gave me a genuine smile.
"It's very nice to meet you," I said.

"Mrs. Luther, we're very pleased that Mr. Luther has married, and we want to make this home as comfortable for you as it is for him."

"Clara, where does Mr. Luther sleep?"

She smiled at me and beckoned me to follow her.

I giggled and tiptoed behind her.

We went all the way down the hall there was a door at the end with three steps leading up to it. She opened the door, and then we walked in.

I was shocked that it was not decorated at all. All of the walls were tan. There wasn't anything on them. He had three identical dark brown dressers, a California king, dark-brown bed, and an oversized rocking chair. His bedding was cream with a huge soft wool blanket and a giant horse on it. I imagined Xavier making love to me wrapped all up in that blanket. I swallowed hard and went back to focusing on his room. I went into his bathroom. And once again, plain on plain.

"Clara, why doesn't he decorate his room?"

"He told me that his wife would decorate it. He said he would want her as comfortable as possible here. Since this is where they would spend most of their time," she laughed aloud, and I joined in.

"Clara, I need your help with a project then."

"Anything for you, Mrs. Luther."

"I need a very big and secret hiding place. Somewhere Mr. Luther would never look."

"I know such a place," she giggled.

We headed downstairs while I admired every nook and cranny. Xavier's house was amazing; everything was made from some sort of wood. We headed into the kitchen for breakfast. There was a spread on a big table like no other: all types of meat, eggs, and pastries. Clara filled my plate and sat me down at a breakfast table right by a window. I ate while she went through some papers on the counter.

"Tell me about him?"

"He's kind. He's very quiet. He's really smart. He's a great boss, and he supports his whole entire family. A man like that deserves the best." I nodded back at her.

"How did this happen between you two?" she asked.

"I met him in a diner, and I fell in love with him on a Ferris wheel."

She gave me a big grin, and then there was a buzzing noise. She excused herself and left the room. I awkwardly sat there, finished my breakfast in silence, and then cleaned my dishes.

I was curious to see the entire house, but I didn't know it well enough to go exploring. So, I went out the side kitchen door to find Xavier. Everyone was friendly and eager to help me find him. One of the staff told me that he was in the brown barn up on the hill. I was walking up towards the barn when Sonic ran up to me. He just sniffed and sniffed before he fell out in front of me again. I had to laugh at him, this time because I was aware of his trick.

"Sonic, why do keep doing that? I see you, silly." I bent down and rubbed his stomach real good and he went bananas.

"You shouldn't have done that. He's going to expect that from you here on out."

I didn't turn around; I didn't need to. I could pick out his voice in a crowd of complete strangers talking. He had a stern, thick voice; it reminded me of honey. I stood straight and Sonic whined and moaned at my feet. I patted him on his head. He licked my hand.

"Can I help with anything around here?" I looked up at Xavier and he was staring at me.

"What do you want to do?" he asked as his left eyebrow rose with curiosity.

"I don't care. I just don't want to mess up anything."

"Are you afraid of chickens?"

"I don't think so… I've never been around one."

"Follow me."

We went down by the brown barn. I saw a long strip of little tiny houses that were fenced in. Xavier handed me a pair of black rubber boots. They were similar to my rain boots but thicker. I took my leather boots off and put on the rubber ones. He handed me a big, wire basket with a cushion at the bottom of it. The cushion had little dips in it. He opened the door and I walked in behind him. There was a wall of little boxes with hay in them. Every last one of them had eggs in it.

"Get the eggs from the empty nest and put them in the basket," he said.

"Okay."

My basket was full in no time. He handed me another and then another. I started paying attention now, and I counted the eggs. There was a spot for twenty-four eggs in each basket. I was on my fifth basket now and I had several more boxes to go. Xavier just leaned against the counter and watched my every move. Normally, when someone watched me like a hawk, it made me feel uncomfortable. But, Xavier watching me didn't make me feel that way. I wanted to do the job right and I wanted him to correct me when I messed up.

"How many eggs are picked up daily?"

"About two hundred or so."

"And then where do they go?"

"To the markets."

"Markets?"

"Grocery stores."

I nodded. "Where are the cartons?"

"We have to clean them first."

When I finished getting all the eggs, he piled all the baskets up on a dolly. I changed my boots again, and then we wheeled the eggs over to a building behind the chicken coop. The steel building was cold like a refrigerator. Xavier handed me a big coat, but he didn't wear one. There were four big machines in the steel building.

"We place the eggs in that tray and then you press this button. This will clean the eggs. Once we're done cleaning them, we will place them in this machine and this will dry them. Once they're dry, we can put them in the cartons, and then they're ready for the stores."

"Wow!"

He grinned at me. "Do you like eggs?"

"Yes, and now I have a whole new respect for them."

There was a buzzing noise followed by someone paging Xavier through the speakers. The announcement said that he had a guest in the main quarters.

He closed his eyes and looked up at the ceiling. "Come on."

"But we didn't finish the eggs."

"Someone else will finish them. Come on." He held his hand out for me, and I took it.

I turned around and looked over at the big machines one more time.

"We can come back and finish them. I won't let anybody touch them," he told me with a smile.

He helped me get out of the big coat. We held hands as we walked back towards the house. I could see a group of people standing next to the red barn. I gripped Xavier's hand a little tighter.

"It's okay. Just pretend like you're in love with me."

I looked over at him with a slight frown and he was looking straight ahead.

"How many of me has it been?"

"What? I've never been married before," he said as he stopped walking to look at me head on.

"I meant, how many girls have you introduced them to?"

"None."

"Oh…"

He turned back around and almost dragged me behind him.

"Xavier," I whispered so he would slow down a little.

He slowed a bit and took in deep breaths.

I could make out the people now. There were eight men and six women. No one had a smile on their faces and that made me nervous.

"They all look mad," I stated aloud.

"Furious."

"Why?"

"Because we eloped."

We were in ear range of them now, so we both kept quiet. One woman stood out from the bunch. She wore a white, buttoned-down shirt with dark denim capris, red pumps, and blood red lips. Her hands were on her hips and her head was cocked to the side a little.

Xavier had squeezed my hand one last time before he greeted them.

"Hello, all. I would like to introduce you to my beautiful wife, Phoebe." They all stared at me. I noticed that one of the women in the back had her mouth wide open.

I grinned and beamed at them all, but only got a few smiles back from the men. Sonic came up to me. He sniffed and sniffed, and then dropped right in front of me. I kneeled down this time and gave him some extra rubs. He was the only one who liked me in this setting and I was taking full advantage of it.

We all ended up back in the house in a lounge room. There were a few couches and a dozen chairs in there. Xavier had a giant TV hanging on one of the walls and speakers in every corner. I sat there rubbing, scratching, and patting Sonic. Everyone was arguing and fussing at Xavier and it was starting to make my head hurt.

One of the women stomped over to me and swatted Sonic on his rump. "Go!" she yelled at him.

Sonic took off out the door.

Her swift movement and angry mood put tears in my eyes. I stood from my chair and headed back towards the kitchen. I probably didn't have to go this way to get back to my room, but I wasn't familiar with the house yet.

"And where the hell do you think you're going?" I heard someone call from behind me, but I didn't turn around.

"Phoebe?" Xavier called after me, but I kept walking.

Clara met me on my up to my room. "Mrs. Luther, you will sleep in Mr. Luther's room now," she whispered to me.

I nodded and kept treading up the stairs. I pulled my boots and socks off and slumped down in the rocking chair. I looked out the big window, and all I could see was a hay field. There were haystacks and bales of hay all everywhere.

I stared out there for a long time before I was interrupted by a knock on the door. I didn't say a word, so the knocker let themselves on in.

He kneeled down in front of me and wrapped his arms around my waist.

"I didn't know what else to do. You didn't remember me, and it seemed like you didn't want to. So, I left you there after I promised you and your friends that I would never do that."

My eyes drifted from him and went back to the window.

Xavier turned my face back to his gently. "I don't have to pretend like I love you." He then pressed his lips against mine and he felt so familiar to me.

His tongue gently caressed mine over and over. His hands squeezed tighter around my waist as he pulled me to the edge of the chair.

"Do you have any idea how much I want you?" he questioned.

"You don't seem like you want me at all."

"I don't?"

I shook my head.

He unbuckled my belt, unsnapped my jeans, and pulled them down. My panties followed and shortly after, he opened my legs wide.

"Are you going to be quiet?"

I nodded frantically.

"Do you promise?"

I nodded again.

He gave me a wicked smile. He kissed the inner side of my thighs. Xavier's tongue pleasured me so that I could barely contain myself. He had done this on our wedding night and I remembered screaming at the top of my lungs. I wanted to scream now, but I knew I couldn't. He kept pulling me deeper and deeper into his mouth. A few minutes later, I started squealing and squirming around.

"Are you about to -- Don't scream," he broke out.

I frowned and shook my head, but I knew I wasn't going to be able to contain myself.

"I need... I need a pillow." I damn near choked trying to keep quiet.

Xavier rushed over to the bed and came back quickly with one. I held onto it tightly. That was when he really started showing off down there. I put the pillow up to my face and I started screaming into it.

"That's my girl."

His soothing words made it worse; my convulsions were coming so hard that I could barely stay up in the chair. I just wanted to slide down to the floor and lay there.

When I was finally back to my conscious self, Xavier carried me to the bathroom. He turned the shower on and helped me undress the rest of the way. I got into the shower and almost begged him to come in there but decided not to. The shower was huge; it had four showerheads that all hit you at once. It was so sensational that I almost had another orgasm from the water beating on my neck and back.

After I was squeaky clean, I shut the rainforest off. I opened the shower door and there was a big fluffy towel sitting on the counter. I dried off and wrapped the towel around me.

I went back into Xavier's room. He was looking at something on his phone. I lathered up with some lotion and put my clothes I had taken off back on; I didn't want any of them to know what we'd been up to. I slid the princess cut back onto my special finger. He watched me briefly, but then turned away as if he didn't want to be caught staring at me.

"It's a really nice ring," I admitted.

"It should be. It cost a pretty penny."

"Sorry."

Xavier smiled at me and I grinned back.

Once I was dressed, he came over and held his hand out for me. There was a sound that sounded much like a cow's bell, and then a clock from outside started chiming.

"What's that?"

"The lunch bell."

"What?"

"Sometimes, we get a little distracted on the farm, so we have to have it to remind us what time it is."

"Is there a dinner bell, too?"

"Yes."

I laughed, and he tugged me on. "Listen, if they start nailing into you again, I'll stop it right away. You don't have to leave me with them all by myself."

"They're your family."

"They're yours, too… well, for the rest of this week they are."

Something in his words stung and made my eyes water a little, but I quickly shook off that sad feeling I was suddenly starting to feel.

We stepped down and entered his dining room. Once again, there was a spread enough to feed an army. I wondered if every meal was buffet style in this house. There was a stack of plates at the beginning of the buffet. We both a grabbed a plate and started piling them full. Xavier's plate was so filled with different foods that it looked like a trough. He waited for me at the end so we could both walk into the dining room together.

There were three tables that sat twelve at each. All of them were full except for two seats, one at the men's table, and one at the women's table. Clara sat with some other staffers at the last table. I stretched my neck to see if there was room to move a chair over there. But, there wasn't and Xavier cleared his throat. I turned to face him. He was standing by the empty chair at the women's table. I swallowed hard and sat down in the empty seat. Xavier pushed my chair up for me and squeezed my shoulder. I patted his hand as he went to sit at his table.

I kept my head down and focused on my food. The women kept the conversation going amongst themselves. I didn't focus any of my attention on any of them. I ate slowly and chewed every single bite thoroughly. When I was full, I just pushed my food around on my plate like a small child. I looked back over at Xavier, and he was done eating as well. I looked over at Clara and she was getting up to collect the finished plates. I got up and gathered my dirty dishes, and then I grabbed Xavier's plate. I went into the kitchen with them and started rinsing them off. Clara came up behind me. "Mrs. Luther, please let me do that."

I gave her a frantic look. She smiled and gave me a nod as if she understood what my eyes told her.

"I'll go collect the rest of the dishes. You just stay right here," she said.

A minute or so later, someone walked in behind me and wrapped his arms around me. "I have something I need to go do. I won't be able to finish the eggs with you, but I have a very good substitute that's willing to take my place." He rested his chin on my shoulder and pulled me tighter to him.

I squealed a little and nodded.

"Give me a kiss."

I leaned back and pressed my lips against his. He turned me around while I was elbow-deep in suds. He pulled me against him and kissed me almost violently. I wrapped my soapy hands around his neck.

Some of the staffers walked through, coughing back their laughs and giggles.

I pulled away from him with a smile, but he didn't share my same amusement. His face was serious and I didn't know why.

He pulled me in closer to him. "Stay close to my momma. She's the only one that matters to me."

I nodded and by looking at his face, I knew he meant it.

"Phoebe, I love you."

I wanted to say I love you back, but I wasn't sure if he would believe me. I touched the side of his face. He closed his eyes. I pressed my lips against his again, but then he pulled away from me. He held onto both of my wrists and I watched him. When Clara walked in slowly with the rest of the dishes, Xavier let go of my wrists.

He turned to walk away and I tugged at his arm. "Can I go with you?"

"I need you stay here."

"Why?"

"It's important."

"I don't want to stay here without you."

"You'll be with me," a loud voice said from around the corner. "I hear you like the chickens." The woman in the button-down shirt and the red heels with the fire engine red lipstick came from around the corner. "We weren't properly introduced earlier and I apologize for that. Mintora Luther, but you can call me Mini."

I looked over at Xavier and he was smiling at the woman. He had given her a kiss on her cheek before he touched my chin. As he walked away, I listened for his boots on the marble floor until I couldn't hear them anymore.

CHAPTER 4

Mr. and Mrs. Luther

"Well, Mrs. Luther, Jr, let's go." I looked over at Clara. She nodded at me with a smile before leaving us alone. I chuckled on the inside at her little nickname for me.

Mini traded her heels for a pair of black work boots. I followed Mrs. Luther, Sr. out to the chicken coop. We went into the steel shed, and Mini put on one of the big coats and then handed me one. She started up the first batch of eggs while I watched her diligently.

"The ones you have to watch out for are Xenophon, Xena, and Xyliar. Xyliar is the closest to Xavier. She is the meanest. She's married to Omni and I'm not sure how he deals with her, but they make it work. They have three children, and they live in Nevada. Xena is my middle girl. She's married to Baxter. They have three children and one on the way. They live on a ranch in Arizona. Xan Jr. is married to Dandrea and they have two children. They live up the street from us. My second son, Xanthus, is married to Kellie. They have four children. They live in L.A. Xandra, my eldest daughter, she's married to Roland, and they don't have any children yet. They live across town from us."

When she spoke of her Xandra, I could see that there was something in her eyes. She was her favorite daughter. And, I had a strong feeling Xavier was her favorite son.

"Xylon and Xenohon are my problem boys. Anytime trouble is nearby, it finds those two. They still live at home and I have a strong feeling they will never leave." She laughed at herself.

I smiled as I just listened and kept working, I felt better moving, so I didn't have to do that awkward staring into her eyes. I looked up at the big clock. It had only been an hour. I wondered how long Xavier was going to be gone. I thought about staying in his room until he came back.

"Phoebe, if I asked you a couple of questions, would you be perfectly honest with me?"

"Yes, ma'am."

"This stays in here, just between you and me."

I swallowed and waited for her questions.

"How did you guys really meet?"

"What did he tell you?"

"A lie," she said sternly. "This will be our little secret and I won't tell a soul," she promised.

I trusted Mini, so I decided to be perfectly honest with her. I started at the very beginning and I didn't leave anything out. After we had cleaned and dried all of the eggs, we sat up on the steel tables. She laughed at all the funny parts and awed at all the sweet parts. I was very animated with her and that made me feel good to be myself. She held my hand when I told her how I knew I loved him on the Ferris wheel.

"How did he propose?"

I told her about how after the Ferris wheel part we went and found one of the many 24-hour jewelry stores.

"May I see your ring?"

I held my hand out for her to see and she gawked at it.

"Wow, that's some ring."

"I know." I stared down at it and smiled.

"I think you guys' story is great and thank you so much for sharing it with me."

I turned away from her and looked over at all the eggs.

"But, I can't help but to wonder how you really feel about him."

"I hurt him badly the morning after… I didn't remember him or anything about the night at all. I tried, but the memories wouldn't come back. By that next morning, I had remembered everything, but I had finally sent him back to his hotel. The last thing I told him was that my lawyer would be contacting his lawyer. I tried to find him when I got my memory back, but he was long gone by then. By the time I got back to work, my godfather, who happened to be my boss and my attorney, had every single thing on Xavier and demanded that I come up here, and convince him to sign the divorce papers."

She stared me down. Then, she started swinging her legs while chewing on the inside of her mouth. "How do you feel about him, Phoebe?"

"It doesn't matter."

"Why doesn't it?"

"It's just my rotten luck."

"But, I think you do love him."

"I don't want any of his money or any parts of this farm. I just need for him to sign my papers, but he said he wouldn't until you guys left."

"Phoebe, have you told him that you love him?"

"He doesn't believe me."

"Oh, honey." She tried to soothe me, but I wasn't in the mood.

"I'm getting a headache. I'm going to go lay down for a while."

"You don't have run off. We can talk about something else."

I gave her a small smile. "Maybe later."

"Honey, I wasn't trying to upset you."

"I know."

She held her arms out for me and I stepped into her embrace. She gave me a triple kiss on my forehead without even removing her lips in between.

Over her shoulder, I saw Xena and Xyliar, two of Xavier's sisters walking towards the steel building. It was a good thing I wanted to go lie down. I didn't make eye contact with either one of them as I walked past them.

At the house, I stepped in through the kitchen and walked right passed Clara. "Mrs. Luther, are you alright?"

"Yes, I just have a light headache. I'm going to go lie down for a while."

"Mr. Luther may be gone a while. I'll bring dinner up to you."

"Thank you, Clara."

"You will do no such thing, Clara."

I heard a voice at the doorframe. I wasn't sure which sister that was, but I was getting the hell out of that kitchen.

"This is your house and no one, not even my pig-headed sisters, are going to keep you locked up in a room upstairs," Xena said.

I walked past her and headed upstairs. I wasn't sure if she was being facetious or serious because her face held a very blank expression. She didn't look mean, but she wasn't smiling either.

I stripped down to my tank and panties before sliding deep under the covers. I drifted off into a deep sleep quickly. I was standing in front of the movie theater in Vegas. There was a mannequin in the ticket booth, holding a ticket for a showing for "A Patch of Blue." I got the ticket out of the mannequin's hand and went inside of the theater. There were mannequins behind the counter and there were even some inside the theater. Some were coupled up and some were by themselves. The theater was packed.

I saw an empty seat in the dead center of the theater. I walked down the crowded row to get to the empty seat. The closer I got, the more I realized that the person sitting next to the open seat was a real person. It was Xavier. He was smiling widely at me. I sat down next to him.

He pulled me into a kiss but then all of a sudden, he stiffened. I pulled back to see what was the matter. Xavier was now a mannequin; the mannequin wore all of Xavier's clothes. I shook him hard and then, the whole scene had disappeared. Everything turned black- pitch black. I screamed and screamed for help, but no one came.

"Phoebe! Wake up! Wake up, baby!" I was jerked and pulled away from the pitch-blackness into the shadows of Xavier's bedroom.

I could see dim lights coming from the hallway.

"Momma, turn on all the lights!" Xavier told her frantically.

"X," I sighed.

"I'm right here. Open your eyes for me."

I heard Xavier, but I couldn't find him.

"Phoebes, open your eyes, baby. Look at me. I'm right here."

I reached for his voice and found him. When I opened my eyes slowly, he was cradling me with the covers tucked around me.

"There you go." He kissed my sweaty forehead.

"How long has she been having night terrors?" His mother asked.

I didn't hear Xavier respond to her. I heard water running, then someone placed a cool towel on my head; it felt so good. Xavier gave me a few quick pecks on my lips. I was so exhausted that I could barely move. I focused on the room now, and all the sisters were there and their father. Mini sat on the bed with Xavier and me. I focused on her face.

She smiled at me and asked, "You think you can eat something?"

I shook my head. I was still a little shaken up from the nightmare.

"What scared you?" Xavier asked.

"We were in the theater, watching 'A Patch of Blue', but everyone else there was a mannequin. And, then you turned into a mannequin… and everything went pitch black. I couldn't see a thing. I couldn't find you anymore."

"I swear, I'll never leave you alone again," Xavier promised me.

None of them probably knew what those words meant to me. But, even I didn't even trust the words that were coming out of his mouth now. Xavier and I both knew this wasn't going to work and this was nothing but a charade for his family. I was about sick and tired of all this pretending, and I just wanted to be left alone. I pulled away from Xavier and snuggled up to a pillow. I buried my face in it and sobbed continuously.

I heard the shuffling of feet walking away from me, and a creak from the door closing as, eventually, the room fell silent. When I raised my head, I was alone, but the bedside lamps were on. I drifted off again, nightmare free this time. By the time I woke again, it was 2:00 a.m. I looked over at the empty side of the bed. Xavier hadn't come to bed yet. I pulled on a robe and house shoes and tiptoed out of the room.

There were a few dim lights on downstairs. I followed them, but still no Xavier. The house was still. I noticed the kitchen door was cracked, so I went outside. I looked across the backyard and saw nothing but the pole lights. I went around to the side of the house and saw a single, dim light. I followed it. The crunching sound under my feet startled me. I was in the hayfield, and there was a lantern up ahead.

"Xavier?" I whispered.

"Phoebe, what's wrong?" I heard him get up quickly as the crunch was now following him.

"Nothing. I was looking for you." He met up with me and held me.

"You didn't come to bed."

"I wasn't sure . . . I didn't know if you wanted me to."

I pushed up a little and kissed him. He kissed me back, but his was a little more needing than mine was.

"Can anyone see us?"

"No," he breathed.

I pulled my robe off and it dropped to the ground. He wrapped his arms tight around me. "I need you."

"Phoebe, do you remember everything?"

"Yes."

"I mean about --"

"I took your virginity. I remember," I said.

"You don't think of me as less of a man?"

"No, why would you think that?"

"Because I'm not that experienced."

"You ate me out like a pro earlier."

"Phoebes."

"It was beautiful, and you're so much of a man inside and out, and those freakishly large body parts . . ."

"I want to please you."

"You do in more ways than one."

"I--"

I interrupted "Shhhh. I love you!"

We had sex right there hidden from the common eye in the hay bells. He wanted me on top of him and he admired my body and my plump bare breasts. So, I rode him for the duration of our lovemaking that night. We got back to the bedroom a little after 4:00 a.m. and we slept in until 9:00. No one came looking for us, no one called for us, and it was nice.

I woke him with him in my mouth. I had to put a pillow over his face this time to keep him from screaming. We made love again in the shower that morning and Xavier was ready for another position. We eased into him taking me from behind and he loved it. We were finally in our honeymoon state; we couldn't keep our hands off each other. We had sex twice in the steel building behind the chicken coop. I loved it when he rammed me across the tables. I sucked him off again in the tractor, way out in the west field. We made love all that night and again that next morning. By the fourth day, we were both worn out, but we were still so hungry for each other.

Xavier's sisters had finally started addressing me as "her" or "hey" but nothing more. I think all of the brothers and brothers-in-law accepted me. I couldn't keep all the kids straight though. There were so many of them. Xavier said they were the "truckload gang."

On Friday night, Xavier wanted to take me for a drive alone. I packed us a blanket and some water. I wasn't sure where this ride would take us and what state we would be in on our way back. We drove for at least thirty minutes and I rode right up under him in his pickup just like the people in the movies. I kissed and nuzzled at him the whole drive.

"Now stop it. You know when you start messing with my ear that's it!" Xavier warned me.

"Pull over then," I told him.

"Not yet. I want to show you something." Xavier told me.

I calmed down a little but not that much. We pulled into a town, and there were city lights and people everywhere. They were walking and laughing.

"Where are we?"

"Tex Tip."

"Oh." That meant absolutely nothing to me.

"It's the closest town city life we have."

"It's really nice. Look at all the shops."

"We may not have the big name department stores you're used to, but we have the means of getting them."

He drove down to a corner lot and cut the truck off. He got out and didn't even bother taking the keys or locking the door. I thought this was the strangest thing, but I stayed quiet. I slid out behind him and we linked hands immediately. He gave me a kiss. I kissed him back, giving him a little tongue.

"Mrs. Luther, if you don't stop, I'm going to throw you down in the truck."

"Um, do you promise?" I teased.

"Come on, my little nympho."

I giggled and we went to the empty shop on the corner. Xavier pulled a key out of his pocket to open the door. He held the door open for me and I walked in while still holding his hand. I held it a little tighter because the room was so dark. He leaned over and switched on a light quickly. "I'm sorry, baby."

I pulled him closer to me and looked the shop over. "What is it?"

"Whose is it?"

"What?"

"I know it doesn't look like a whole lot right now, but baby, picture racks and racks of clothes you like. And, I was thinking that you should have two registers over there and we'll have to build the dressing rooms… But, the storage in the back is huge and there's an office plus two bathrooms."

"Xavier, was it this?"

"Your boutique."

I continued to look the room over. Then, it finally registered. He wanted me to stay and he knew that I always wanted a boutique of my own. I felt like he was trying to trap me because he wanted me to have a whole truckload of kids. He wanted me to be his little lady, who hung on his every single word. That just wasn't going to happen.

I tried to unhook our hands, but Xavier wouldn't let me go.

"Phoebes?" He looked terrified as hell of me, and I knew I had to get out of there before I crumpled.

"We had an agreement," I said.

"What?"

"You told me you'd sign the papers when your family left. Are you trying to renegotiate with me?" Xavier gave me one of the guiltiest looks I had ever seen.

I turned away from and stomped away.

"Phoebe, baby, please don't run from me." He ran to me and wrapped his arms around me, but I jerked out of his grip.

"Stop it!" I spat through my teeth.

I folded my arms tightly around me as I paced back and forth across the hardwood floor.

"Phoebes, let's just go home, and we'll discuss this later."

"You know what? That's the best idea you've had all week. I need to go home."

"Wait, what do you mean?"

"You know exactly what I mean!"

"Phoebe, you're not leaving me!"

I said nothing to him as I stared out of the front window.

"Baby, just forget about Boutique. I was doing it for you. I thought you--"

I walked past him, out the front door, and stomped over to the truck. I opened the passenger door, got in and slammed the door shut. I leaned my body all the way up against the door so I could be all the way on the passenger's side. I knew I was being childish, but I didn't give a damn right now. There would be no more sitting up under him anymore. I stared straight ahead. That's when I noticed that there were twinkly lights above the shop. The sign read *Phoebe's Corner*. I cringed and turned my head, putting my attention on the passenger's window.

He slowly locked up the store and hopped into the truck. We rode back in complete silence. When we made it to the beginning of his road, he pulled over.

"Phoebe, I'm sorry I didn't mean to make you feel, umm, however you're feeling."

I opened the truck door and got out.

"Phoebe! Where are you going?"

"I'm staying at the resort tonight. Have someone bring me my things tomorrow."

"Baby, please don't do this!"

I kept walking back towards the resort on the corner. He got back in his truck and turned it around.

"Baby, get on in the truck now. It's dark out here. Let's just go home and get in bed. We can make love all night and morning. We can fix this, Phoebes." He followed me all the way to the resort, begging and pleading with me, but I never budged. Once I got through the front doors, I heard tire squealing and gravel flying.

CHAPTER 5

Meow Meow

I woke the next morning to a tapping at the door. I rolled over in the same clothes I had on last night. I stumbled to the door and looked out the peephole. I refreshed my ponytail and tried to rub in the tear streaks from my face. I opened the door.

"Good morning," Mini greeted me.

"Good morning."

"May I come in?" She asked.

"Yes, ma'am." I moved back so she could enter.

She sat down at the little table and I sat across from her.

She looked me over before giving me a small smile. "You look just about the same as he does." She set her keys down on the table and intertwined her fingers. "I told him he pushed you too hard. Of course, he doesn't understand because he's a man and that would be too much like right if he did."

I leaned over on the table and crossed my arms under my chest. She reached for my hands. I held them out and she took both of them in hers. She bent over and kissed the top of my ring finger. When she looked up at me, tears were falling from her now pink eyes.

"He's never loved anyone like how he loves you. I was so scared for him for years. He's dated and dated, but he never found that special one. And, my God, he found such a beautiful woman inside and out in the filthy streets of Vegas. You know when he told me he wanted to build his clientele base, I tried to stray him away from Vegas. But, he said he had a feeling about it, and now I know that feeling was you."

"I can't do this with him," I sobbed.

"Honey, I know you're scared, and he's terrified of you as well. I believe you two are meant to be, but maybe you need more time to soak it all in. You're both hanging by a thread and you both need a little healing. Don't give up on him, Phoebe. I've taught him all that I can. I know I have to let him go and be a man, but he's my favorite, my baby. No matter if you leave today or tomorrow. Don't sign those papers yet. You guys still need time."

I nodded.

She kissed the top of my hand again before releasing me. She stood from the chair and walked past me, heading for the door.

"Phoebe, could you do me a favor?"

I looked over at her without answering.

"Please don't leave without giving him a proper goodbye." I nodded as she opened the door. "I'll be downstairs. Take all the time you need."

I went into the bathroom, scrubbed my face, and brushed my teeth. I went downstairs to check out. Pauline and Ben looked sad and told me that they hoped to see me again. I gave them both smiles and told then I would recommend their resort to all my friends.

I went outside. Mini was in a big red pickup. I jumped in and we headed for the farm. When we pulled up, Sonic and Boom, both came running up to us.

"Why are they named Sonic and Boom?"

"Xavier was big into this cartoon where this guy used to say Sonic Boom to get his special powers or something like that."

I nodded as Sonic fell out in front of me, as he liked to do. "Oh, get up, you big faker," I scolded him.

He whined and howled until I rubbed his belly good.

"You've got him spoiled," Mini told me.

"I know. He's a big ole baby."

Just then, Boom, who had never come up to me before, wandered over and licked the inside of my palm. I patted him on the head, and he stayed right by my side.

I walked into the front of the house. All of the men was in the front room, well, all of them except for Xavier. They all watched me silently and didn't make eye contact with anyone.

I walked through the house, headed straight upstairs, walked in the room, and it looked like a bomb had just hit. There was shit everywhere. I rushed over to the armoire and packed as fast as I could. I didn't believe Xavier would ever put hands on me, but from the looks of this room, I wasn't sure. I heard a commotion from downstairs and that made me start packing even faster.

Someone was running up the stairs with loud heavy thuds and my heart stopped. Someone was angry. I ran behind the closet door and hid when the footsteps got closer to the room.

Xavier started yelling my name. "Phoebe!"

I cringed and wrapped my arms around myself. Xavier burst through the bedroom door. I heard what sounded like other footsteps behind him, but he slammed the door shut in front of them. Whoever it was, started beating and pounding on the door at once.

"Open the door, bro!"

"Xavier, open this door right now!" I heard Mini say.

I was too afraid to say anything because he didn't know I was standing behind the closet door. He walked slowly to the two bags on the floor that I had been filling up. I took two quick steps towards the door and I had just touched the doorknob when he swung around. He looked at me with a confused face, and I froze.

"Are you leaving me?" he asked me in the softest tone I've ever heard from him.

"Xavier, we already talked about this."

"But we've--" He broke off.

"You know I have to go."

"Because your Uncle says so."

"Don't do that."

"What? Don't do what? Tell the truth! Well, here's a little fucking truth for you, wife of mine." He stomped over to me and yanked me by both of my shoulders. "You made me fall in love with you. I let my guard down with you. I fucking married you and then, I gave you something no one on Earth had ever gotten from me… you treated me like shit. You don't care anything about me. I don't like the sober girl you're portraying. I want the shit-faced drunk one back. She let me see the real her and she didn't have all these walls up." He shook the shit out of me and shoved me away from him.

I went to the door and frantically tried to open it.

"Oh, no the hell you don't. Get your shit. Get all your fucking shit out of my house!" He pulled me over to my bags

I just dropped to the floor and cried into my hands.

"Phoebe! Open the door, Honey." Hearing Mini's voice just made me cry harder.

Xavier was throwing my clothes and jewelry at me. He kept ranting and spat out horrible things about me.

"Clara the key now!" I heard Mini yelling.

"You're going to be by your fucking self for the rest of your miserable life! You came alive when you met me, and you know it. All of your friends say you're a wishy-washy, stuck-up bitch! And, I should have known that I didn't have a chance. They said you lose all interest in a man as soon as you sleep with them. I should have just left you all hot and bothered. Maybe you would have begged me to stay. And, what are you rushing home for? You have no one but that fucking cat and she doesn't even like you. Where are your friends? You haven't talked to any of them since you been here!"

I sat there in silence and listened to everything he was saying. He was still in his ranting and raving stage, pacing the bedroom, looking like a crazed lunatic.

I felt a tap on my shoulder and turned around slowly. Clara and Mini stood there reaching for me. I placed my hand in theirs, and they helped me up. Xavier was throwing shit everywhere. He went into the bathroom and started emptying the draws in the cabinets. They slowly walked downstairs with me and everyone watched us. All the brothers, brothers-in-law, sisters, and sisters-in-law gawked at me leaving the house.

"What about her stuff?" Clara asked Mini.

"I don't want it," I whispered.

They nodded and we walked through the quiet house.

"What the fuck!" I heard Xavier yelling from upstairs.

"Help her into the truck and then lock the doors," Mini told Clara.

Mini released my forearm and headed back into the house. Clara got me to the truck and I was getting in when Xavier caught me.

"Wait!" he breathed hard. His chest was going up and down and up and down so hard.

I slid the princess cut ring off my special finger and handed it to him. I leaned over and kissed him on the cheek.

"Goodbye," I said, as I saw the tears welling up in his eyes.

"What are you going to do?" he asked me in a calmer voice.

"Go home and get ready for work Monday."

"What am I supposed to do?" He whispered in that sweet tone from before. I reached my hand to him touching the side of his face.

"You're going to do the same." He pulled me to him and pressed his forehead against mine, and I let him.

"Can I drive you?"

"No."

"Did you love me?"

"I still love you."

"Baby, don't leave me."

I kissed his lips and he kissed me back.

"I gotta go."

He backed up a little. I pulled the door shut. Three of the guys put my bags in the bed of the truck. Mini opened the driver's side and handed me my purse.

"You just go on and leave then. This boy gave you everything he had and you just crumpled it all up. I hope you cry yourself to sleep at night. I hope you suffer badly for this," Xan Sr. yelled out to me.

"Xan Sr.!" Mini called out to him.

Everyone watched us now. Staffers watched from the sides of the house, and all the family stood in the front yard. I could hear the children playing in the backyard.

"I don't believe this. Boy, you ain't do nothing? Your wife is leaving you!" Xan Sr. yelled to Xavier.

"Let them be, Daddy." I heard one of my brother-in-laws call out to him.

"You hush. You just hush up and let me mourn for my son's heart," Xavier's father spit out.

Mini got in the driver's seat and we drove away from the big farm.

**

When I finally made it home that evening, I went over to Caress' to pick up Meow Meow. She met me outside in the driveway.

"Hey, Caress, I came to pick up the little monster." I sighed.

"Honey, James wouldn't let me call you and bother you, but poor little Meow Meow passed away two days ago."

That was the final straw. I dropped to my knees and let everything out of me. I screamed and cried for hours. I ended up on Caress' couch that day, the next, and the next. Uncle James told Caress that if I didn't show up for work by Tuesday that he was going to come to get me himself.

I went home that night and threw all of Meow Meow's little trinkets away. I couldn't help but think she probably died of a broken heart. I was a horrible owner and she knew it.

My mailbox was full on the house phone. I didn't know where my cell phone was. When I got to work the next morning, Caress told me my mailbox was full and that she'd been taking messages for me. I apologized to her for the inconvenience and she told me it was nothing. She had given me my messages before I went into my office. Most of the messages were from Addison and Daphne. I just wasn't in the mood to talk to either one of them. I had one from my mother and I gave her a call back.

"Hello," she answered.

"Hi Mom."

"Well, I haven't heard from you in a while and I thought I should call and check on my child."

"How are you guys?"

"Why don't you come and see?"

"I sure will, this weekend."

"Good. How are you weathering?" she asked.

"Oh, it's always foggy in San Francisco."

"I meant you."

"I'll heal. I always do."

"You seem to be doing a lot of that lately."

I just held the phone, not really knowing what else to say at the moment.

"Alrighty, so we'll see you this weekend, right? You need some sun in your life," my mother probed.

She would use any excuse to get me to Los Angeles with her and dad.

"Right."

"See you then."

"See you."

My phone buzzed and Caress' voice came through the speaker.

"Phoebe, James would like for you to come to his office."

"I'm kind of in the middle of something. Could you ask him if --"

"Tell her to get in here now!" I heard him yelling from his office through the receiver.

"I'm on my way." I got up and went down the hall to his office.

Everyone watched me as I walked into the heart of the firm. Caress gave me a small smile and I returned it.

I knocked. He gave the "You may enter" look.

I sat down right across from him. He was on the phone, talking. I kept my head to the floor. He tossed an envelope in front of me so I opened it. I slid the contents out and gasped at what I saw. Xavier had signed the divorce papers and had given me my ring back. I felt the tears welling up. I knew I couldn't make it without crying in front of Uncle James. I straightened the divorce papers and placed them on top of the envelope. Then, I placed the ring in the center of the divorce papers. I made sure everything was straight and neat before I got up to walk to the door.

"Hold on a sec, John. Come back here!" he called out to me.

"I need to use the restroom," I told him without turning around.

He didn't try to stop me.

I walked to the bathroom. I shut and locked the main door as soon as I was inside. I didn't want anybody in here for this show. After a few minutes, there was a knock, and I knew it was Caress. I scrubbed my face and dried it well. I opened the door and she stood back so I could come out.

"James had a meeting across town, so he won't be back for the rest of the day."

I nodded and did my best not to sniffle.

"Go home, and we'll see you tomorrow."

I left the office and went straight home to bed. Mr. Luther's wish came true: I did cry myself to sleep every single night. Getting out of my bed was getting hard and harder.

The next few months were terrible and seemed to drag by. We celebrated me passing the bar, me winning my first case, and my birthday. A few co-workers and college friends came to celebrate with me. Mom, Dad, Caress, Uncle James, Addison, and Daphne were the ones who planned the festivities. We had half of the restaurant reserved for our party.

Caress and I went to the bathroom together. At the bathroom sink, we laughed and poked fun about who was drunker. Someone walked in the bathroom and we tried to keep our voices down to a minimum.

"Well hello, Mrs. Luther."

Caress and I both turned to see who had called me that.

Mini and Xyliar stood by the bathroom door. I yanked a few paper towels out of the dispenser and tugged for Caress to come with me. I walked past them. Caress stared at me as I tugged her away with me.

"Phoebe," Caress uttered.

"Shhhh."

"Phoebe!" she yanked at me, and I finally looked at her.

"I don't want to talk about it. Let's just go!"

"Well, you better get ready to talk about it." I followed her frightened eyes and they were glued to our table.

I noticed the people standing up around it and then, I saw him. He was standing toe to toe with Uncle James and my father. The restaurant was so noisy that no one could hear them, but if you were looking at them, you could see the tension in their bodies. We slowly walked over to the table and when I got within earshot, I couldn't believe what I was hearing.

"You were just a toy to her and she's done playing with you. Why don't you stay in the toy chest like a good little puppet?" Uncle James spat.

Xavier pushed Uncle James. He lost his balance a little, falling back and bumping into the table hard; a few glasses clinked and broke from the jolt. Now everyone in the restaurant was looking at our scene.

I stepped over in front of Uncle James while he collected himself. I glared at him and his eyes looked as if they lost their fight. My dad stared at me with confusion and shook his head at Uncle James. Mom stood to her feet and told Dad she was ready to go. Dad moved over towards her quickly while they both stared at me.

"I'm sorry," I told them both with glossy eyes.

"I can't believe you would hide this from us, Phoebe," my mother told me with a hurt face.

"It's extremely complicated."

"Did you need money that badly? It couldn't have been love; you don't even love yourself," Dad said.

I stood there, looking at them and then, I stepped back so they could pass through.

"I'll take care of the bill," Uncle James said as he chugged down the rest of his drink. He straightened his suit coat and walked away from the table.

I looked over at the rest of the party still sitting there in shock. I had to say something. *Quick, anything to fill up this thick air,* I thought to myself.

"Thank you all so much for coming out to celebrate my birthday with me. My apologies for the confusion and for the embarrassment of knowing me," I said with tears streaming my face.

Addison and Daphne stood. They both looked as though they would fight a war for me. I shook my head at the both of them. I had squeezed Caress' hand before I grabbed my clutch bag from the table.

I turned, passing the Luther men and women. Xavier just stood there staring at me as I walked passed him. I went out of the front door and did not look back. I was waiting for a cab when I heard the front door of the restaurant open. A cab stopped and I climbed in and gave the driver my address. I threw my head back against the seat. I knew it would take at least thirty-five minutes to get home. I powered my phone off, knowing it was going to be ringing all night, and let myself lose consciousness. When I got home, I got straight into the shower then collapsed in bed.

I woke with a jolt when the doorbell buzzed. I heard the buzzer again and looked over at the clock. It was a little after midnight. I got up, checked the street, and saw a cab out front.

"Yes?" I spoke into the box.

"May I come up?" he asked me in that honey voice.

I pressed the buzzer. I unlocked the door and went back to the window. The cab was driving away.

He walked through the door and I stepped into his view.

"What are you doing here?" I barked.

He walked to me after he shut and locked the door behind him. He pulled me to him, and I surrendered my whole body and soul to him just like that.

"Xavier," I breathed as he traced little kisses down my throat.

I couldn't keep still with him distracting me like this. He pulled back to the window seat and sat down, pulling me over the top of him. He had changed from his suit and was now wearing a fitting tee with loose jeans. His biceps ate through his shirt. I wrapped my hands around his big, cut arms.

"Xavier," I breathed as he slid his hands under my sleep tee.

"Did you miss me?"

I nodded, not able to speak. I yanked one of his hands and forced it down below.

"Mmm," he moaned.

"Take me," I begged him.

He put his lips on mine and I took over with a force that had him nearly breathless.

"Slow down, Mrs. Luther."

I pulled back and stared at him. "Say it again," I moaned.

"Mrs. Luther," he said, pushing my panties to the side, sliding two of his fingers in me.

"Oh God, again!"

"Mrs. Luther."

"Don't stop!"

"Mrs. Luther."

"I want you, X."

"I'm right here."

"You're not close enough… Get inside me."

"No."

"Why not?"

"We're not ready for that yet."

"What?! Xavier, you have three full fingers in me. What are you talking about?"

"Shhhh."

"Fuck this," I said.

"Do you want me to stop?"

Just then, he rolled his thumb across my pulsating knot. My eyes rolled back to the back of my head.

"Do you?"

"Uhmmupha," was all I could mumble out.

He stood and laid me on my back on the window seat on top of the cushion.

"No, no don't stop," I told him frantically.

"Shhhh." He bent down and started his liquid late night snack.

"Oh God, yes!" I arched my back and pumped myself towards his mouth. He wrapped his arms around my waist and really got into it.

"Xavier!" I said a little too loudly.

I scared myself with my reaction. I put both hands on the back of his head and forced him to stay. He dropped to his knees, growled, and slurped me up. He stayed down there until I came twice. My legs shook and they felt like gelatin. I stayed lying down on the window seat too afraid to move. He wiped his mouth and stood. He looked around, taking my condo all in.

"It's a lot smaller than your palace, but I like it," I told him half-heartedly. He looked at all the framed art and looked over every piece of décor I had.

"Would you like something to drink? I have water, juice, beer, vodka, wine, and a bottle of champagne…"

He just shook his head and continued to look over the place. I had a two-bed, two-bath condo; there wasn't a lot to see here, but he seemed fascinated.

"Where's Meow Meow?"

Hearing his thick, honeyed voice made my mouth water.

"She passed away four months ago," I told him, not meeting his eyes.

"I'm sorry."

"So, when you said all I had was my cat, well, I don't even have her now." I gave him a smile that didn't reach my eyes.

He came and sat down next to me. "Do you want a divorce?"

"What kind of marriage do we have? We haven't seen each other in four months."

"We can have whatever kind of marriage you want to have. But, do you want to divorce me?"

"I don't know."

That was the honest truth. I had no idea if I wanted to divorce him or not.

"Would you do me one last favor?"

I looked at him, not budging.

"I want to give you a million dollars and I want you to quit or take a long leave of absent from the firm. I want you to do whatever you want to do with the money. Go wherever you want to go and be whoever you want to be. Once you're done, I want you to call me and let me know if you want to divorce me or not. If you want this divorce, I will give it to you. But, to be perfectly honest with you, Phoebe, I don't think you really know what you want."

"Xavier, what do you want?"

"I want you, but I want you to want me, too."

"I do."

"Not the way I need you to."

We sat there in silence, both of us looking out the window.

"Do you have a passport?" he asked.

"Yes."

He touched the side of my face. "I'm sorry for the scene at the restaurant, but you just act as if I never even existed."

"It's okay… I think about you all the time. I couldn't stomach turning the divorce papers in. They're in my bank safe," I told him.

Xavier nodded.

I really didn't hold any grudge against him. I understood his pain and I understood his reactions.

"You look just like your mom."

I nodded. "Can I sleep next to you?"

"Yes." He gave me his hand.

I guided him behind the French doors and into my bedroom. I lay down and he slid in behind me. I pressed my butt up against him and his not-so-little morsel.

"Don't," he warned.

I rubbed up against him harder and he moaned. "X, it's been so long."

"I know."

"Don't you want me?"

"I wouldn't be here if I didn't."

"Take me."

"No."

"I'm *your* wife."

"Then, show me."

CHAPTER 6

Where Are You Now?

My flight landed at Kingsford Smith's International Airport. I had been out of the country before but only to Canada and Mexico. Now I was in Sydney, Australia and I was exhausted. It took me two days to get used to the time change. I had four days left to enjoy this beautiful country. My first adventure was to visit the Royal Botanical Gardens. I took a tour and ate at the famous Botanic Gardens Restaurant. I did some site seeing and then, that evening, I went and watched Swan Lake at the Opera

House. When I got back to the hotel room, I was exhausted, but I had sworn to Xavier that I would send him an email about my day each evening.

Xavier,

First off, I have to say thank you for this. I know I've just started this journey of self-appreciation, but I love it already. I've never really appreciated flowers before. Yes, I've bought them for birthdays and I've owned a plant or two, but to learn and appreciate their beauty and purpose is a whole other ballgame. I think you should plant some Plumeria Rubra out front. They're called the Intense Rainbow and that kind of reminds me of us. I've seen just about every flower and plant that grows in Australia. And, I saw Swan Lake at the Opera House; it was amazing. Now it's time for bed, so I can wake bright and early and enjoy the rest of this beautiful country. Now here's a big kiss for you from me, down under...

Yours Truly,
Phoebe

Phoebe,

I know you're good and asleep now, but I'm so glad you had a good time today. I hope you see everything that Sydney has to offer you. Sonic and Boom say hi and that they miss you. Momma is coming down to spend some time with me for a couple of weeks. Clara says to bring her a souvenir from each city you visit. She said she could see the world through your eyes. I have another favor to ask of you. I know you're still working on one, but I have another. I can't help it; I'm a very greedy man. Please send me pictures of you daily. I want to see if that beautiful smile can get any bigger. I love you, Phoebe, and I miss you terribly.

Always,
Xavier

The next few weeks were absolutely amazing. I had been to four different countries and six of their major cities.

Xavier,

I had the best time today. I ate at a small café around the corner from my bed and breakfast, and I met a plus-size fashion designer. I'm apparently staying in a fashion district, and I had no idea. We sat and talked for hours, and then she insisted I come back to her studio. She measured every inch of me and was determined to have a beautiful gown made for me before I leave on Saturday. It's so beautiful here. We'll have to come back here one day. It's so romantic, and it's so quiet here you can really think. I didn't know how much I appreciated quiet, but I do. I walked by a horse stable, and I couldn't do anything but think of you. I miss you so much, and I can't wait to see you.

Love,
Phoebe

Phoebe,

It sounds like you're having a blast and I'm happy for you. Momma is still here and I don't think she's leaving anytime soon. I wonder if she and Dad had an argument. She's never stayed this long before, but it's nice to have her around. I hired a new hand by the name of Jamie to help with the horses. Jamie and I went to buy a few more horses today. I really think I want to get into racing the horses and maybe even get a few show horses. Jamie knows all about that stuff. Apparently, back in the day, Jamie used to do all of that with the horses. I think that tomorrow we're going to look at some better stalls, and maybe, a few more possible upgrades for the stables. I think I'm going to keep Jamie on full-time; I could really use the help. I can't wait for you guys to meet.

Always, Xavier

Xavier,

I had lunch with a seven kids today. I couldn't resist; they kept staring at me from a side street. The poor things were begging for money and food. I had the waiter go over and bring them chairs so they could sit. After thirty minutes of our lunch, people from the restaurant ended up coming over. They all wanted to give the children money, and everyone wanted to pay for their food. The owner of the restaurant put our lunch on the house. I couldn't believe one small act from me caused a commotion. I felt good and made a lot of friends today. I don't know how many times I can thank you. Xavier, you have changed my life more than you'll ever know. My eyes used to be shut. Now, they're wide open. Thank you for making me and my life better.

Love,
Phoebe

Phoebe,

You don't have to thank me. Just reading your joyful words on my computer screen is thanks enough. I can so image you with a truckload of kids. I think that would really be a good look for you (hint hint). I know how you can bring out the best in people. I'm not surprised at all by the acts of the others in the restaurant. Today was not one of my best days. But, hearing about your very eventful day makes mine a little more tolerable. We lost three sheep this morning. Someone did not secure the gate correctly, and some coyotes got in. The herdsmen that live the closest to the sheep shot one of the coyotes, but the other four got away. I'm going to get a double fence put up this week for extra protection. I slept through the whole thing. I'm ashamed to say that I sleep with a couple of your garments tucked around a pillow. I think of you a lot, and this helps me sleep. Until your next email.

Always,
Xavier

Xavier,

I am so sorry about the sheep. I'm sorry I'm not familiar enough with the farm to know how much damage this is. I think the double fence is a great idea. I wasn't sure what a coyote was. I looked it up one on the Internet, and it scared the shit out of me. Now, I see why you have the complete property surrounded by fences. Do they ever come up to the house? Now I fear for Sonic and Boom. You have a really big house, Xavier. No wonder you didn't hear anything. I'm sad about the sheep now, and I wish there were something I could do. How is Clara, and do you ever see Mr. Ben and his wife from the resort? Please tell everyone I said hello and that I wish everyone well. Sweet dreams, and until the next.

Love,
Phoebe

Phoebe,

I didn't mean to bring you down. Baby, when you live on a farm, this sort of thing happens. They started on the fence today and said it will take three days to finish. The coyotes go where they can find food. This is the second or third time they've made in the gates, but they only made it in because someone forgot to shut a gate. Our gates are well secured, and if one of them got too close to the house, Sonic and Boom would smell them. As for

Sonic and Boom, they are too old and way too mean for anything to eat them. I saw Mr. Ben and Pauline down at the farmers' market the other day. They asked about you and so did about a hundred other people. Word has spread like wildfire that I got married to some big shot lawyer from the city. People aren't normally so nosey around these parts, but I think they're all excited for me. Everyone wants to meet you and they want to know what kind of clothes you're going to sell in your boutique. I told everyone who asked that you're on a fashion world tour. I told them you're getting hands-on experience and one-on-one conversations with some of the biggest fashion gurus. Clara is fine. She told me to tell you that she misses you and to hurry home. But I say you take all the time you need. I'll be waiting for you right here on the farm.

Always,
Xavier

Xavier,

Today was an extremely eventful day. I watched an authentic Roman toga being made. It was amazing and so beautiful. Rome is different; everyone here seems so hard as a rock. And their native tongue is so beautiful. To stand in front of the Coliseum and the Vatican just took my breath away. I wish you were here enjoying all if this with me. Everything here seems so sturdy and strong. During the tour, the guide even seemed mesmerized by everything she showed us. There were two families on the tour from California. We chatted it up for a while. Tell Clara I have some recipes for her to try out. Check the attachment; I uploaded some pictures. Until the next.

Love,
Phoebe

Phoebe,

I bet you enjoyed every bit of that toga making. It sounds fun, and I bet they used the best fabric out there. I know the Coliseum and the Vatican looks beautiful on TV. I can't even imagine being up close and personal to them. I got all of the pictures, and they are all amazing. Next time, let someone take a picture or two of you in the pictures. I would love to see your beautiful face and your beaming smile. I'll tell Clara about the recipes, and I assure you she will be grateful. She loves trying new things and to have a recipe all the way from Rome, she'll flip. Jamie has been out sick for the past two days. I didn't know things would get so backed up with the horses. I'm going to have to hire a couple more people for the horse training and attending. I'm really enjoying prepping the horses for the shows and racing. Until the next.

Always,

Xavier

I had been hinting around for weeks to Xavier and the man wasn't biting. I wanted him to come join me on my extended vacation, but he didn't. I knew exactly what I wanted out of life and I knew whom I wanted to spend it with. Xavier was my husband and I planned to keep him that way.

I had just emailed Xavier last night and told him I had just arrived in Italy, which was a tiny lie. I wanted to surprise him and I wanted to tell him face to face what I wanted. I drove down the long rock road and pulled up to the Iron Gate.

Mrs. Luther's voice came through the box. I told her I had a delivery and she buzzed me in. When I drove up, I waited for Sonic and Boom, but neither one of them came. I got out of the car and walked up to the front door. I knocked, and Mrs. Luther was wiping her blue-stained hands on an apron.

"Thank you, Jesus!" she yelled and then yanked me into a bear hug. She pulled back and popped me with the dishrag. "Where in tarnation have you been? Wait... Are you here to stay?"

I smiled wide and nodded.

"I knew it!" she squealed and pulled me into the house.

"Clara!" Mrs. Luther yelled through the house. "Clara!" she yelled some more.

Clara came jogging into the front room and stopped.

"Oh my word!" She rushed over to hug me and kiss both sides of my face.

"Clara, she here to stay," Mini crooned.

Clara widened her eyes and started yelling in Spanish.

Three young girls came running from the kitchen. One got my keys from my hand and the other two ran up the stairs.

"What are they doing?" I asked.

"Xavier hasn't slept in your bedroom since that horrible day. He said if you came back that he'd go back in there."

"Oh Honey, it's been almost a year," Mini said.

"I know, but I'm all straightened out. I'm ready to see my husband. Where is he?"

"You know he's out back, somewhere. Go on now." She shooed me out the door.

"Mother Luther?"

"Mini," she corrected me.

"Mini, why have you been here so long?"

She gave Clara a look and pushed me out the door, without meeting my eyes. I wasn't going to push her for the answer, so I walked out to the barns and he wasn't in there. I asked one of his farm hands and they told me he was in the haystacks. Something inside me jolted, and I all of sudden, I felt almost sickly from my nerves. I was so excited to see Xavier that I was almost obsessed with him wrapping me up in his arms.

I kicked my shoes off once I reached the haystacks. I wanted to surprise him completely and my shoes crunching on the hay would give me away. I almost made it to the haystack clearing; I could hear someone singing softly in the distance. I walked even more carefully and the voice got even clearer. Someone was singing a slow love song. She sang about a lost love and starting over with someone new. I could see the clearing now as I peeked around the corner. I was shocked from the site before me.

There was a pretty, thin, blonde sitting down in between Xavier's legs. She was singing and he was French braiding her hair. He touched her with love and affection. I could see it and feel it.

"Ouch!" she laughed.

"I'm sorry, Jamie," he laughed back to her.

I turned and took off running. I had to get out of there, and I had to leave right now. I passed Clara at the entry of the haystacks. She was holding my shoes and I didn't even stop to get them. I ran to the front of the house and one of the girls was pulling my purse out. I slowed and yanked my purse and keys away from her.

I jumped in the car and heard Mini calling for me from the porch. I started the car and took off for the gate. I saw Xavier and Jamie running to the front of the house in my review mirror. I sat at the gate until it whined open slowly. Sonic and Boom were both barking and running after the car now.

I just kept going through the gate and I floored it down the long country road. When I made it to the highway, I rested my head on the steering wheel and lost it. I was so stupid to think he would actually wait on me. He was a man and he had needs- needs that I wasn't here to give him, but Jamie was here. There was a tap at the window and I jumped in shock.

Ben was standing outside my passenger side window. "Mrs. Luther?"

I turned back toward the highway and floored it. I didn't know where I was going and I didn't care. All I knew was I had to get away from Xavier and that damn farm. I eventually made to a small community. I looked at the sign. It read Tex Tip and that made cry even harder. I drove down the wide road and pulled up in front of Phoebe's Corner. I sat there and cried and cried.

Nothing ever works out for me; I will continue to be a screwed up, I thought to myself.

Now that I didn't have a job and I had no idea where I was going to live. I guessed I was going to have to go back to my parent's house. I thought about it and that just made me feel worst.

I put my head back on the steering wheel and had a hysterical moment. I don't know how long I was like that, but when I rose up from my episode, there was a figure right standing right next to me. I focused on the plaid shirt and then on the bulge in the seat of the wranglers. I'd know that bulge anywhere.

He pulled the door handle and it was locked. He stared at me with pink-tinted eyes. I pushed the unlock button and he yanked the door open. He gently pulled my left leg out and he squatted down between my legs. He laid his head on my thigh and he awkwardly wrapped his arms around my waist and seatbelt. I cried a little more and he just held on to me.

I felt so pathetic that I wished I could find a hole and just crawl into it and die.

"It's not what you think," he whispered.

I didn't respond to him right away; I just sat there. A few people walked by, but they didn't even stare. They just glanced and kept on going. That shocked me. In Los Angeles, there would have been a crowd with their cell phones out recording us. They would have been waiting for a fight and would have posted it within seconds, but not here. Everyone seemed to mind their own business.

"I want a divorce," I told him.

He sat up and stared at me with glassy eyes.

"Phoebe, don't leave me. My life doesn't make sense without you." He pulled me tighter, and I turned away from him. He stretched up and kissed the side of my wet face. "Please, babe. Don't leave me."

"You love her; I can see that. I'll be fine. You don't have to feel sorry for me anymore," I said with my head facing the passenger side window.

"Will you come take a ride with me?"

I turned back towards him and he kissed me quickly. He acted like his life depended on it and that he had to do it now or never. I kissed him back and savored his taste. He pulled away and stood. He reached his hand out for me and I took it. He helped me out the car and into his truck cab. We drove about five minutes away from town and turned on a side road. We pulled up to a brand new, two-story cabin. The grass in the front yard was well manicured and there were two wooden rocking chairs on the porch. Xavier left the lights on the truck, came over to my side and opened the door. I slid out into his arms so that we could walk around to the front of the truck.

"I built this for you. If you're working late and don't feel like coming all the way home or if you just need to get away from me, this is your home away from home if you want."

I tried to take it all in.

Xavier turned me around and looked at me square on.

"Jamie is a lesbian and she has a girlfriend. They've been together for six years now. She was teaching me how to braid long hair for the show horses I purchased. There is absolutely nothing between her and me. I swear to you on everything that I love."

He was serious and I believed every word that left his lips.

"I did everything but beg you to come to me and you didn't budge."

He stared at me for a long moment. I shifted my eyes away from him and stared out into the distance.

"Look at me," he whispered.

I looked back at him.

"Tell me how you feel…"

I stared at him and said nothing. I noticed it was getting harder for me to breathe. Xavier placed both of his hands on the sides of my face. He made me stare into his eyes and then, I knew what I had to do.

"I want you."

"Okay."

"Right now, Xavier."

He pulled me back to the truck cab. I yanked my jeans and panties off. He killed the truck's engine and unzipped his pants. I slid over on top of him and he stopped me when I sat down on him.

"Tell me, Phoebe," he said with a sexy growl.

Xavier had to hear me say how I felt about him. "I love you, Xavier."

"Yes, yes Phoebe," he started panting and frowning.

I realized quickly that Xavier needed me as much as I needed him.

"I don't have any condoms on me."

"And I'm not on the pill."

We both looked at each other again. Both of us were panting and in need of each other's bodies.

"Do you want babies?" he asked me.

"Yes, a whole truckload of them," I told him.

"Now. You want to start now?" He asked me.

"Why not? I've already seen the world. How about you?"

"And, I've seen it through your eyes." He told me.

Xavier pulled his big, one-eyed snake free and I surrendered myself to him.

I rode him until the cows came home and I meant that literally. There were over a dozen cows walking through the pasture on the side of the house. It was pitch black dark now. I sat on top of Xavier, all ooey gooey and sticky. I knew with all the semen he had shot in me that I'd be pregnant. He held on to me and I held him.

"I don't want to leave here."

"We don't have to. I mean, we will eventually need to eat and change clothes, but we have hot and cold running water in there. There are a few of mother's quilts in the master bedroom closet."

"Really?"

We ended up staying at the house for four more days. We didn't need any clothes, but the food issue began to be a problem. Mini called on our first day to check on us and Xavier told her where we were. Two hours after that phone call, we had a huge basket on the porch with a ton of food, the bare necessities, and lounge gear. We had breakfast, lunch, and dinner waiting on us in a basket for the next four days. When we finally emerged from the house and headed back towards town, Xavier turned his signal on to turn into the shopping area.

"No," I protested.

"Your car?"

"Send someone back to get it," I said all snuggled up against him.

We acted like two young teenagers in love riding in the truck cab all up under each other. When we pulled up to the house, no one was in site, and we went upstairs to put on some decent clothes. Once again, he took me in the shower as he had for the last four days.

"Mr. Luther, you have the stamina of a teenager."

"Mrs. Luther, I have years of catching up to do."

"Well, by all means, Mr. Luther, have your way."

"Why thank you, Mrs. Luther. I will."

We left our bedroom at dinnertime and ended up snuggling up on one of the loveseats in the great room. Mini and Clara walked in and paid us no mind. Mini handed me a big red book, a blue book, and a white book. I looked over at Xavier, and he smiled while he enjoyed his newspaper. I opened the red book and it was the staff's schedules and their information. The blue book was the breakfast, lunch, and dinner schedule. And, the last book,

the red one, was the finance book. I slammed it shut
quickly when I saw the balance that was in the bank. I had
never seen that many numbers on one line my life.

"Why did she give these to me?" I whispered.

"You're the woman of the house now," he said,
then kissed the top of my forehead.

"You trust me with this stuff?"

"I trust you with my heart and without my heart, I
wouldn't have a life. So, I trust you with my life."

"I want you."

"Shhhh, let's eat dinner first, and then, we'll go to
bed early," he said in a whispered laugh.

Xavier and I went on like rabbits for the next two
months.

Xavier started his horseracing and showing business
with his pure breeds. I opened my boutique, and soon after,
I had to open two more locations. Xavier and I lived part-
time in the house closer to town. He would go to work on
the farm. I would go to work at the boutique. We would go
home and spend our nights in bed for a while until we got
the news.

I had passed out at the Boutique on a Wednesday
afternoon in the spring. Xavier met me at the hospital in the
ER. Xavier had called our family doctor to meet us at the

E.R. Dr. Patterson patted Xavier on the back and told him he was supposed to keep the fertilizer in the field. We found out that I was three months pregnant and I never knew the wiser. I had been working all day and then making love to my new husband all night. I hadn't even realized I hadn't had a period for months. Two months later, Dr. Patterson told us we would be having a bouncing baby boy. We soon moved to the big house full time for some help. Then like clockwork, one bouncing baby popped out, one after the other.

Six months after Xavier Jr. was born, we found out about the upcoming arrival of Xilla. After her, there was Xander. Last and definitely not least, we had the twins Xeraphina and Xadrian. They were hell on wheels. Xadrian came out screaming, and he's been doing it ever since.

I decided to keep the whole X tradition when it came to the children's name. Xavier and I now had our very own truck full of kids. As soon as I got one out, Xavier was filling me with another. I had to admit that I loved being pregnant. Xavier loved taking care of me.

I reconciled with Uncle James and he came down to visit us every chance he got. Addison and Daphne were the best godmothers a child could ever want. I now had six locations and I named the stores after each child. We were so busy now with the farm and the boutiques that we rarely had a second alone. There were always paws or little hands tugging at us at all times. When the grandparents or godparents came to visit the kids, Xavier and I got to stay at our house in town. We also went there on other occasions, birthdays, anniversaries and whenever we could get a sitter. We liked to go there so we could have that hot balls deep kind of sex.

One evening after paying a small fortune for a sitter and giving a lame excuse to the kids, we went to the house in town. We just lay in each other's arm in the silence for hours.

"I was thinking. I would like to build the kids a Ferris wheel."

I looked over at my husband, who had the exact same stamina he had the day we got married. His eyes were tight and his wrinkles on his forehead were visible, he was thinking hard and deep.

"I don't know about the kids, but I sure would love one," I told him.

He gave me a wide smile. "I didn't think I could love you anymore than I already did, but each and every day you make me."

I thought about our wedding night so long ago. Xavier and I were dancing in the little white chapel. We were waiting our turn to get hitched. We danced to Whitney Houston's *I Wanna Dance with Somebody*. We were so drunk that we had a slow swing instead of an upbeat tempo. We had stopped at three other chapels, but I told Xavier that I refused to let Elvis marry us. We found this chapel and it was Elvis free. When we finally made it to the aisle and up to the podium, Xavier kissed me a dozen times all over my face.

"Phoebe, I don't think I can love you anymore than I do right now." He kissed me for the very first time as his wife.

The memory faded and I smiled. "I'm glad I didn't divorce you," I admitted, pulling myself back from our wedding day.

"And, I'm glad you decided to play strip date with me."

"I'll play strip date with you anytime, Mr. Luther."

"How about now? Mrs. Luther?"

"I'm already naked."

"Strip bed then," he said with a smile.

I laughed aloud and he rolled on top of me and slid into me. That was when the beginning of our new game started; we liked to call it "Strip bed."

40137529R00083

Made in the USA
Middletown, DE
23 March 2019